LONG RIDE HOME

Also by Louis L'Amour in Large Print:

Chancy
Conagher
High Lonesome
The Key-Lock Man
Killoe
Kiowa Trail
The Mountain Valley War
Radigan
Reilly's Luck
Silver Canyon
Valley of the Sun
War Party
Mojave Crossing
The Sackett Brand

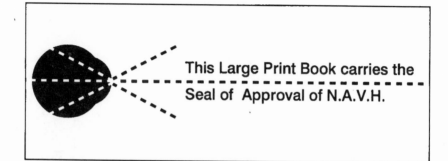

This Large Print Book carries the Seal of Approval of N.A.V.H.

LONG RIDE HOME

Louis L'Amour

G.K. Hall & Co. • **Thorndike, Maine**

Published in 1998 by arrangement with Bantam Books, a division of Bantam Doubleday Dell Publishing Group, Inc.

G.K. Hall Large Print Western Series.

The text of this Large Print edition is unabridged.
Other aspects of the book may vary from the original edition.

Set in 16 pt. Plantin by Al Chase.

Printed in the United States on permanent paper.

Library of Congress Cataloging in Publication Data

L'Amour, Louis, 1908–
   Long ride home / Louis L'Amour.
    p. (large print) cm.
   ISBN 0-7838-1954-4 (lg. print : hc : alk. paper)
   1. Western stories. gsafd. 2. Large type books. I. Title.
  [PS3523.A446L645 1998]
   813'.52—DC20   96-36267

Contents

Author's Note

THE CACTUS KID PAYS A DEBT

I have written several stories about the Cactus Kid. In this case some of the activity takes place in San Francisco. Bull-Run Allen was a known man on the Barbary Coast and vicinity and his place at the corner of Sullivan Alley and Pacific Street was notorious. One-Ear Tim was also known and his ear was said to have been chewed off during a physical arbitration with an unwilling robbery victim.

The Barbary Coast was known for its dives and for its multitude of ways of relieving innocent victims of their funds. However, once in a while they picked on the wrong man. The odds were against anybody with money, and the sooner one got away from the area, the better.

Many of the tough joints along the water-front were built over the hulks of old ships sunken in the bay to enlarge the land area. Most of the dives had a convenient trap-door for the disposal of surplus bodies or through which shanghaied sailors could be taken by boat out to a waiting ship. It was not unusual; for a sight-seer to have a drink in such a dive and wake up on a slow boat to China. It was often a one-way trip.

THE CACTUS KID
PAYS A DEBT

Four people, two women and two men, boarded the San Francisco boat in company with the Cactus Kid. Knight's Landing was a freight landing rather than a passenger stop, and the five had been drawn together while waiting on the dock.

Mr. Harper, pompous in black broadcloth, wore muttonchop whiskers and prominent mustache. Ronald Starrett, younger and immaculate in dark suit and hat, looked with disdain at the Kid's wide white hat, neat gray suit and high-heeled boots.

The Kid carried a carpetbag that never left his hands, a fact duly noted by both men and one of the women. The Kid, more at home aboard the hurricane deck of a bronc than on a river steamer, had good reason for care. He was taking fifteen thousand dollars, the final payment on the Walking YY, from his boss, Jim Wise, to old Macintosh.

"What time does this boat get in?" the Kid asked of Harper.

"Around midnight," Harper said. "If you haven't a hotel in mind, I'd suggest the Palace."

"If you go there," Starrett added, "stay out of the Cinch Room or you'll lose everything you have."

"Thanks," the Cactus Kid responded dryly.

Five feet seven inches in his sock feet, and a

compact one hundred and fifty-five, the Kid, with his shock of curly hair and a smile women thought charming, was usually taken to be younger and softer than he was.

On the Walking YY and in its vicinity the Kid was a living legend, and the only person in his home country who did not tremble at the Kid's step was Jenny Simms — or if she did, it was in another sense.

"It's a positive shame!" the older woman burst out. "A young man like you, so nice looking and all, going to that awful town! You be careful of your company, young man!"

Nesselrode Clay, otherwise the Cactus Kid, flushed deeply. "I reckon I will, ma'am. I'll be in town only a few hours on business. I want to get back to the ranch."

Harper glanced thoughtfully at the carpetbag and Starrett's eyes followed. The younger woman, obviously a proud young lady, indulged in no idle conversation. Miss Lily Carfather was going to San Francisco with her aunt, somebody had said.

"It looks like a dull trip," Starrett's voice was casual. "Would anybody care for a quiet game of cards?"

Mr. Harper glanced up abruptly, taking in the young man with a suspicious, measuring eye. "Never play with strangers," he replied brusquely.

"I think," Lily Carfather said icily, "gambling is abominable!"

10

"On the contrary," Starrett defended, "it is a perfectly honorable pastime when played by gentlemen, and we are gentlemen here."

He drew out a deck of cards, broke the seal and shuffled the cards without skill. The Cactus Kid considered Ronald Starrett more carefully.

Harper glanced at his watch. "Well," he mumbled, "there is a good bit of time. . . . A little poker, you said?" He glanced at the Kid who shrugged and moved to the table.

"If," Starrett glanced at the women, "you'd care to join us? Please don't think me bold but — a friendly game? For small stakes?"

Lily Carfather dropped her eyes. "Well —" she hesitated.

"Lily!" The woman was shocked. "You wouldn't."

"On the contrary —" her chin lifted defiantly — "I believe I shall!"

Ronald Starrett shuffled the cards and handed them to Harper for the cut. No limit was set, the Kid noticed, as play began. Picking up his cards the Kid found himself with a pair of jacks.

The Cactus Kid had lost his innocence where cards were concerned in Tascosa when he was sixteen, and as this game proceeded, he grew increasingly interested. He stayed even, while his observant eyes noted that the end of the middle finger on Starrett's hand was missing. Also, Mr. Harper played a shrewd and careful game, while behind the seeming innocence of Lily Carfather

11

was considerable card savvy.

Suddenly the Kid found himself holding three nines. He considered them, decided to stay and on the draw picked up a pair of jacks. He won a small pot. And he won the next two hands.

"You're lucky, Mr. Clay," Starrett suggested, smiling. "Well, maybe we'll get some of it back later."

The Kid drew nothing on the following hand and threw in, but on the next he won a fair-sized pot. He found himself feeling a little like a missionary being banqueted by cannibals. He lost a little, won some more and found himself almost a hundred dollars ahead. He was not surprised when Starrett dealt him four kings and a trey. He tossed in the trey, drew a queen and began to bet.

After two rounds of betting, Harper dropped out. Starrett had taken two cards as had Lily. On the next round, with both the Kid and Lily raising, Starrett dropped out. On the showdown Lily had four aces. She gathered in the pot, winning more than a hundred dollars from the Kid alone.

Harper dealt and the Kid lost again, then Lily dealt and the Kid glanced at his cards and tossed them into the discard. The fun was over now and he was slated for the axe. When it came his turn to deal, he shuffled and easily built up a bottom stock from selected discards, passed the cards to Lily for the cut, then picked up the deck and shifted the cut in a smoothly done movement and proceeded to deal swiftly, building his own hand from the bottom until he held the three he wanted.

Harper threw in his hand but Starrett and Lily stayed. The Kid gave Starrett three, Lily two, and himself — from the bottom — two. Picking up his hand he looked into the smug faces of a royal flush.

Lily glanced at her hand. "I want to raise it twenty dollars," she said sweetly.

"I'll see that and raise it ten," the Kid offered, "I feel lucky."

The pot built up until it contained almost four hundred dollars. Starrett called with a full house and Lily followed with a small straight. Coolly, the Kid placed his royal flush on the table and gathered in the pot.

Harper bit the end from his cigar and Lily's face grew pale, her eyes very bright. Starrett's face flushed dull red and his eyes grew angry. "You're very lucky!" he sneered.

It was Starrett's deal and the Kid knew it was coming right at him. And it came, starting with three aces. Coolly, he tossed in his hand and Starrett fumbled a card.

Lily smiled icily at the Kid. "What's the matter?" she asked, too sweetly. "Not lucky this time?"

"I'm a hunch player," the Kid lied, "and this isn't my hand."

Twice in the next hour the Cactus Kid realized they had him set for the kill, but he avoided it by throwing in a hand or making only an insignificant bet. Harper was a little ahead but Starrett was in the hole for more than six hundred and Lily had lost just as much. The Cactus Kid was over a thousand dollars a winner.

Suddenly, the Kid realized that Lily's aunt was no longer with them. Even as the thought came to him, she returned to the room. "I was worried," he said. "I was afraid you had taken my luck with you."

The aunt's eyes met Lily's and Lily glanced around the table. "Is anyone else thirsty?" she asked. "I am — very!"

"Let's call a waiter and have a few drinks," Starrett suggested.

The Kid nodded agreement, gathering up the discards. There had been an ace in those discards and Harper had held two kings. Now if — He palmed the ace and two kings and slipped them into a bottom stock. Riffling the cards he located another ace and king, adding them to the stock. Then with swift, practiced movements he worked up two good hands for Starrett and Harper. He won again.

Starrett's polish was gone now and when he looked at the Kid, there was hatred in his eyes. Harper said nothing at all, but glanced thoughtfully at Lily.

The drinks were brought in and as they were placed on the table the Kid fumbled a chip, and in grabbing for it knocked over Lily's drink. The Kid sprang to his feet.

"Oh, I'm very sorry, Miss Carfather!" he exclaimed. "Here," he sat down and moved his own glass to her, "you're the thirsty one. Take mine."

Her eyes blazed with fury. "Keep your drink!" she flared. "I won't take anything from you!"

The Cactus Kid grinned suddenly. "No," he agreed, "none of you will."

Their eyes were on him, hard and implacable. "It was too easy," the Kid said cheerfully, "Starrett with that bobbed middle finger. It makes a bottom deal easier but it's a dead giveaway."

With his left hand he pulled the money toward him and began to pocket it. Their eyes, hot with greed, stared at the gold coins.

"I'll be damned if you take that money!" Harper's voice burst out low and hard.

The Cactus Kid smiled his charming, boyish smile. "Stop tryin' to work that derringer out of your pocket, Harper. I've got a Peacemaker in my hand under the table, an' if you feel like gamblin' on a .44 slug, start something."

Harper's gun was out, but he pointed it at Starrett. *"Don't!"* he barked. "Don't start anything, you fool! You want to get me killed?"

"He wouldn't care much, would he, Harper? They'd just have one less to split with."

With a swift, catlike movement, the Cactus Kid was on his feet, his gun covering them all. "Put that derringer in your pocket, Harper. You might get hurt."

His face red, Harper shoved the gun into his

pocket. "All right, you got our money. Why don't you get out of here?"

"One thing yet," the Cactus Kid smiled, "an' maybe I'll hate myself for this, but I did hear her say she was thirsty. Lily, you drink my drink."

"Why — why." She sprang to her feet. "I'll do nothing of —"

"Drink it," he insisted. "You ordered it for me. Try your own medicine."

"I won't! You'd never have the nerve to shoot a woman! You wouldn't dare!"

"You're right. I wouldn't want it on my conscience, and threatening to shoot one of your friends wouldn't help. I think you'd see them both die first. No, there's a better way. You drink it or I'll turn you over to the Vigilantes. I hear there's some around again."

Her frightened eyes went to Starrett. "Drink it, Lily," Starrett said carefully. "We don't dare have them after us. You know that."

She stared at them with pure hatred, then picked up the glass. "I'll kill you for this!" she fairly hissed at the Kid. Then she downed the drink.

His eyes on them, the Kid stepped quickly back to the door, taking his carpetbag with him. Closing the door behind him he ran on tiptoes to the bow of the boat and down into the fo'c'stle. A tired and greasy sailor was tying his shoes.

"Look, mister," the seaman said, "this isn't —"

"I know it," the Kid produced a gold eagle,

16

"I'll give you this for the use of your bunk until we dock and if you forget you saw me."

The seaman got up, grinning. "I'm due on watch, anyway. That's the easiest twenty I ever made!"

The Cactus Kid sat down to think. Obviously they had known he was carrying a large sum of money and had planned to get it away from him with the cards. He had outsmarted them and then spoiled their attempt to dope him. After what he had just done they would make a play not only for the money but for his life as well.

The Cactus Kid frowned. Four sharp operators had not chosen him by accident, but so far as he knew only Jim Wise and old McIntosh knew what he was carrying. It was preposterous to think that either might be involved in this.

Easing out of the bunk, the Kid crept up the ladder and looked out on deck. He froze into stillness in the shadows. A burly, sweatered figure was standing near the bulwark a little aft of the companionway. As this man waited another came up and spoke to him. It was Harper!

So they had hired thugs on the boat. Feeling trapped, the Kid returned to the bunk to consider the matter. Opening the carpetbag he took out his other Colt, strapped the holster under his armpit, and tied it in place with piggin strings.

Finally he dozed, then slept. Awakening with a start he heard the sounds that told of coming alongside the dock and knew they were in San Francisco. Acting on a sudden inspiration, he worked swiftly with the contents of the carpetbag. When he was satisfied he walked boldly out on deck and headed for the gangway. Harper spotted him and spoke to the thug beside him.

None of the poorly lighted streets that led away from the dock looked inviting, but a four-horse carriage marked PALACE HOTEL stood waiting for prospective guests, and the Kid made for it. He was surprised to find Starrett in the carriage, for he had believed he was the first person down the gangway. The driver, a burly ruffian with a red mustache, glanced sharply at the Kid, then let his eyes move to Harper, who stood near a pile of packing cases. Harper nodded.

Other men crowded into the carriage, among them two huskies, and the Kid at once became alert.

The carriage swung into one of the dark streets, then turned into a cross street between high, unlighted buildings. One of the huskies reached up and took down the Palace Hotel sign. The other one looked at the Kid and grinned.

"Pull up!" Starrett ordered. "This is far enough!"

The Cactus Kid left his seat with a lunge, springing to neither right nor left as they probably expected, but straight ahead. He landed astride the nearest horse and with a wild Texas yell kicked with both heels. All four of the frightened animals lunged into their collars and took off down the cobbled street with men shouting and grabbing for holds behind them.

Slipping from the back of the horse to the tongue, the Kid worked his way forward to the lead team. The driver was trying to fight the horses to a stand, but the Kid reached and grabbed the reins. With a vicious jerk, he pulled them loose, and the driver, over-balanced, fell from his seat to the cobblestoned street. The horses picked up speed and ran wild, eyes rolling, jaws slavering.

The Cactus Kid heard the crack of a pistol and a shot went by his ear. Gripping the hip strap with his left hand, which also clutched the carpetbag, the Kid took a chance shot under his arm. Several of the riders had dropped from the rig but the others made a solid block that could scarcely be missed.

A yelp of pain sounded behind him and several men sprang from the carriage. Shoving the pistol into his waistband, the Kid swung astride the off lead horse and hauled desperately on the reins. As the carriage slowed he slid from the animal's back to the street. He scrambled up and ducked into an alley.

Someone yelled from the carriage as it rattled by, and a dark figure loomed in the alley and shouted a reply, then started for him. The Cactus Kid palmed his six-shooter and fired. The charging man fell on his face and the Kid wheeled and ran.

He ducked in and out of alleys until he was winded. Then a door showed suddenly, and he tried the knob. Miraculously, it was not locked and he stepped in, closing and barring it behind him. Feeling his way up dark stairs he new from the faint sounds of tinny music that he was in a building that housed some kind of resort.

On the second floor landing he tried a door, but it was locked so he went on to the third floor. A door opened into a hallway with doors on either side. Swiftly, the Kid hurried down the hall to the head of another flight of stairs. A beefy man with a red face and a walrus mustache stood there.

"Hey!" he demanded roughly. "Who'd you come up with?"

"I came up the back stairs," the Cactus Kid replied, "and I'm going down the front stairs."

"Yeah?" His eyes traveled over the Kid from the broad hat to the carpetbag. "Yeah? Well, we'll talk to Bull Run first."

"Who's Bull Run?"

"Bull Run?" The thug was incredulous. "You ain't heard of Bull Run Allen?"

Something turned over inside the Cactus Kid. He had heard many cowhands and others talk of the BULL RUN, at the corner of Pacific Street and Sullivan Alley. It was one of the toughest and most criminal dives in a town that could boast of many of the worst in the world. He could not have found his way into a worse trap.

"No need to talk to him," he said. "All I want is to go through. Here —" he took a coin from his pocket — "say nothing to anybody. I had

20

some trouble back in the street. Had to slug a gent."

The thug looked avariciously at the money. "Well, I guess it ain't none of my —" His voice broke and he gulped.

The Cactus Kid turned and found himself facing an elephant of a man in a snow-white, ruffled shirt with diamond studs. His big nose was a violent red, his huge hands glittered with gems.

"Who's this?" he demanded harshly. "What's goin' on?"

The thug swallowed. "It's this way, Bull Run," he began to explain. As he talked Allen nodded and studied the Kid. Finally he dropped a huge hand to the Kid's shoulder.

"Put away your money, son," he said genially, "and come wit' me. In trouble, are you? Couldn't have come to a better place. Law doesn't bother my place. I tell 'em you work for me an' it's all right. Let's go to my office."

Seating himself behind a huge desk, he grinned at the Kid. "Cattleman, hey? Used to figure I'd like that line my own self, but I got tied to this joint and couldn't get away. But I make plenty."

He bit the end from a black cigar and leaned forward, his smile fading. "All right, you got away with something good. Just split it down the middle and you can go — and you'll not be bothered."

"You've got me wrong, Allen," the Kid protested. "I've nothing of value. They fired me back on the ranch so I figured I'd come to town. Lost all I had, about fifteen bucks, to some gamblers on a boat. I slugged one of them an' got part of my money back, but they'd already divvied up."

Bull Run Allen scowled. "Describe the gamblers," he ordered.

At the Kid's description his eyes narrowed. "I know 'em. That gent who called himself Harper was Banker Barber, one of the slickest around here. Starrett — I can't figure that play. Starrett works society. He only plays for big money."

Suspicion was alive in his eyes as he studied the Kid. Seeing it, the Cactus Kid gambled. "Say, maybe that explains it! They were hunting somebody else an' got me by mistake! They seemed to think I had money, tried to get me to bet higher. Shucks," the Kid smiled innocently, "I've never had more'n a hundred and twenty dollars at one time!"

Bull Run Allen was not convinced. He wanted a look inside that carpetbag. On the other hand this youngster might be telling the truth and while they talked a rich prize might be getting away.

Bull Run stepped to the door and yelled to a man to send up One-Ear Tim. The manager and bouncer was a burly character with one ear missing and a scarred face.

"Get hold o' the Banker," Bull Run ordered. "I want a talk with him." He grinned at the Kid as Tim walked away. "Now we'll find out about this here."

The Cactus Kid got to his feet. "Sorry I won't

have time to wait," he said. "I'm heading for the Palace Hotel. You can see me there."

Allen gave vent to a fat chuckle of amusement. "Don't think I couldn't," he said, "but you sit still. We'll talk to the Banker first."

"No," the Kid replied quietly, "I can't wait." In his hand he held a .44 Colt. "You come with me, Bull Run. Only you go first."

Allen's eyes grew ugly. "You can't get away with this!" he sneered. "I ain't goin' nowheres, so go ahead an' shoot. No durned kid can —" he lunged, both hands spread wide.

The Cactus Kid was in his element. He struck down Allen's reaching left and smashed the barrel of his Colt over the big man's ear, and Allen hit the floor as if dropped from a roof. Quickly, the Kid stepped outside to the balcony. Still clutching the carpetbag with his left hand, his right hovering near the butt of his .44, he walked down the stairs to the brawling room below, crowded with gamblers and drinkers.

Almost at the door he ran into Tim. The bouncer stopped him. "Where you goin'? The boss wanted you to talk to the Banker."

"He wanted the Banker himself," the Kid said shortly. "Hurry it up, he's already sore."

Tim stared hard at him, but stepped aside, and the Kid walked out into the dark street. Turning left he walked swiftly for a dozen steps then crossed the street and ducked into a dark alley. A few minutes later he arrived at the Palace Hotel.

It was broad day when he awakened. While he bathed and shaved, he thought about his situation. Whoever had tipped the Banker and Starrett to the fact that he carried money must have been close to MacIntosh.

Two attempts had been made to get the money from him and it was likely that two groups now searched for him, only now both groups not only wanted the money but to kill him as well. Allen would not take that pistol blow without retaliation. He dared not — not in this town.

In a town where a man could be murdered for a drink, where it was the proud boast of many that "anything goes," daylight would not end the search for him. Allen had not been boasting when he said his reach included the Palace. So, figure it this way: Bull Run Allen knew where he was. He would know within a matter of minutes of the time the Kid left the hotel. Even in such a fine place as the Palace was, men could be found who would give information for money.

The Kid's safest bet was to get word to MacIntosh that he had the money, then make contact somewhere away from his business office, which might be watched. He checked his guns and returned them, fully loaded, to their places and walked into the hallway, carrying the bag.

A man in a brown suit sat at the end of the hall. He glanced up when the Kid stepped out, then, apparently unconcerned, went back to his paper and turned a page.

The Cactus Kid walked briskly along the hall. Around the corner, he sprinted to the far end and ducked down the back stairs, taking the first flight in about three jumps. Walking the rest of the way more slowly, he stepped out of the back door when the janitor's back was turned. Entering the back door of another building he walked on through to the street and boarded a horse car.

A roughly dressed man loitered in front of the building where MacIntosh had his office, and when the Kid got down from the car the fellow turned and started down the street, almost at a run. The Kid grinned and walked into the building and down the hall to the office door. MacIntosh's name was on the door but he hesitated. If they were waiting for him elsewhere they might also have men planted here. Glancing around, he spotted a door marked *Private*. Taking a chance he opened it and stepped inside.

A big-shouldered man with a shock of white hair and a white, carefully trimmed beard looked up. He was about to speak when the outer door opened and a girl stepped in, Her eyes went wide when she saw the Kid and she stepped back hastily.

"Lily," he exclaimed, and started forward.

Before he could get halfway across the room that door opened again and Banker Barber stepped in. His jaw was hard and his eyes cold. He held a gun in his hand. He motioned toward the carpetbag. "I'll take that!" he said sharply. "Drop it on the floor and step back!"

The Kid knew from his eyes that the Banker would shoot. He also guessed he was more anxious to get the money than revenge and would not shoot in this building unless necessary. The Kid dropped the bag reluctantly and moved back. The Banker took a quick step forward and grasped the handle. Backing away, he unsnapped the top and thrust his hand inside. Keeping his eyes on the two men he drew out a thick sheaf and glancing quickly, his eyes came up, hard with triumph. Dropping the packet back into the bag he snapped it shut.

"Thanks!" he said grimly. "It was worth the trouble!"

"Be careful that Bull Run doesn't take that away from you," the Cactus Kid advised. "He has this place watched and he knew I came here."

"Don't worry!" the Banker replied grimly. "He won't get this! Nobody," he added, "gets this but me." He backed to the door and opened it. "I'd like to know who taught you to bottom deal. You're good!" He stepped back through the door. "And don't try to follow me or I'll kill you."

He jerked the door shut. There was a thud, a grunt, and something heavy slid along the door. Then there were running footsteps. Outside in the street there was a shout, a shot, then more running feet.

MacIntosh leaned back in his chair. "Well," he said testily, "I'm not taking the loss! The money was still in your possession! I'm sorry for Jim Wise, but he still owes me fifteen thousand dollars!"

With a cheerful smile the Cactus Kid went to the door and pulled it open. The body of Banker Barber fell into the room. His skull was bloody from the blow that had felled him, but he was still alive.

"Down in the street," the Kid said, "somebody was just shot. I'm betting it was Starrett. And in a few minutes Bull Run Allen will be cussing a blue streak!"

"He got the money," MacIntosh said sourly, "so why should he cuss?"

The Cactus Kid grinned broadly. From his inside coat pocket he drew an envelope and took from it a slip of paper. He handed it to MacIntosh. "A bank draft," the Kid said complacently, "for fifteen thousand dollars! This morning after I slipped away from them, I went to the Wells Fargo and deposited the money with them. Now make out the receipt and I'll make this right over to you."

Old MacIntosh chuckled. "Fooled 'em, did you? I might have known anybody old Jim Wise would send with that much money would be smart enough to take care of it. What was in the bag?"

"Some packets of carefully trimmed green paper topped with one dollar bills," he said, grinning. "It cost me a few bucks, but it was worth it."

27

MacIntosh chuckled, his eyes lively with humor. "I'd like to see Bull Run's face when he opens that carpetbag! He fancies himself a smart one!" Then he sobered. "You called that girl by name. You know her?"

"She was with them on the boat," the Kid explained. "She even got into the poker game when they tried to rook me. She's good, too," he added, "but she must have been the one who tipped them off. It had to be somebody who knew I'd be carrying money. Who is she?"

"She's been working for me!" MacIntosh said angrily. "Working until just now. I never did put no truck in women folks workin' around offices but she convinced me she could help me and she didn't cost me no more'n a third what a man cost!"

"With a woman," the Cactus Kid said, "it ain't the original cost. It's the upkeep!"

BAD PLACE
TO DIE

Chapter 1

After the rifle shots there was no further sound, and Kim Sartain waited, listening. Beside him Bud Fox held his Winchester ready, eyes roving. "Up ahead," Kim said finally, "let's go."

They rode on then, walking their horses and ready for trouble, two tough, hard-bitten young range riders, top hands both of them, and top hands at trouble, too.

Their view of the trail was cut off by a jutting elbow of rock, but when they rounded it they saw the standing, riderless horse and the uncomfortably sprawled figure in the trail. Around and about them the desert air was still and warm, the sky a brassy blue, the skyline lost in a haze of distance along the mountain ridges beyond the wide valley.

When they reached the body, Kim swung down although already he knew it was useless. A man does not remain alive with half his skull blown off and bullets in his body. The young man who lay there unhappily at trail's end was not more than twenty, but he looked rugged and capable. His gun was in his holster, which was tied in place.

"He wasn't expecting trouble," Bud Fox said needlessly, "an' he never knew what hit him."

"Dry-gulched." Kim was narrow of hip and wide of shoulder. There were places east and south of here where they said he was as fast as Wes Hardin or Billy the Kid. He let his dark, cold eyes rove the flat country around them. "Beats me where they could have been hidin'."

He knelt over the man and searched his pockets. In a wallet there was a letter and a name card. It said he was JOHNNY FARROW, IN CASE OF ACCIDENT NOTIFY HAZEL MORSE, SAND SPRINGS STAGE STATION. Kim showed this to Bud and they exchanged an expressionless look.

"We'll load him up," Kim said, "an' then I'll look around."

When the dead man was draped across his own saddle, Kim mounted and, leaving Bud with the body, rode a slow circle around the area. It was lazy warm in the sunshine and Bud sat quietly, his lean, rawboned body relaxed in the saddle, his watchful gray eyes looking past the freckles of his face. He was wise with the wisdom of a young man who never had time to be a boy, yet who still was, at times.

Kim stopped finally, then disappeared completely as if swallowed by the desert. "Deep wash," Bud Fox said aloud. He got out the makings and rolled a smoke. He looked again at the body. Johnny Farrow had been shot at least six times. "They wanted him dead. Mighty bad, they wanted it."

Kim emerged from the desert and rode slowly back. When he drew up he mopped the sweat from his face. "They laid for him there. Had him dead to rights. About twenty-five yards from their target and they used rifles. When they left, they rode off down the wash."

"How many?" Bud started his horse walking, the led horse following. Kim Sartain's horse moved automatically to join them.

"Three." Kim scanned the desert. "Nearest place for a drink is Sand Springs. They might have gone there."

They rode on, silence building between them. Overhead a lone buzzard circled, faint against the sky. Sweat trickled down Kim's face and he mopped it away. He was twenty-two and had been packing a six-gun low on his leg for seven years. He had started working roundups when he was twelve.

Neither spoke for several miles, their thoughts busy with this new aspect of their business, for this dead young man across the saddle was the man they had come far to see. The old days of the Pony Express were gone, but lately it had been revived in this area for the speeding up of mail and messages. Young Johnny Farrow had been one of the dozen or so riders.

Both Sartain and Fox were riders for the Tumbling K, owned by Ruth Kermit and ramrodded by Ward McQueen, their gunfighting foreman. One week ago they had been borrowed from the ranch by an old friend and were drifting into this country to investigate three mysterious robberies of gold shipments. Those shipments had been highly secret, but somehow that secret had become known to the outlaws. The messages informing the receiving parties of the date of the shipment had been sent in pouches carried by Johnny Farrow. Five shipments had been sent, two had arrived safely. Those two had not been mentioned in messages carried by Farrow.

The mystery lay in the fact that the pouches were sealed and locked tightly with only one other key available, and that at the receiving end. Johnny Farrow's ride was twenty-five miles which took him an even four hours. This route had been paced beforehand by several riders, and day in and day out, four hours was fast time for it. There were three changes of horses, and no one of them took the allowed two minutes. So how could anyone have had access to those messages? Yet the two messages carried by other riders had gone through safely. And the secret gold shipments had gone through because of that fact.

"Too deep for me," Fox said suddenly. "Maybe we should stick to chasin' rustlers or cows. I can't read the brand on this one."

"We'll trail along," Kim said, "an' we got one lead. One o' the hombres in this trick is nervous-like, with his fingers. He breaks twigs." Sartain displayed several inch-long fragments of dead greasewood. Then he put them in an envelope and wrote across it, FOUND WHERE KILLERS WAITED FOR JOHNNY FARROW, and then put it in his vest pocket.

Chapter 2

Ahead of them were some low hills, beyond them rose the bleak and mostly bare slopes of the mountains. Higher on those mountains there was timber, and there were trailing tentacles of forest coming down creases in the hills, following streams of run-off water. The trail searched out an opening in the low hills, and they rode through and saw Sand Springs before them.

The sprawling stage station with its corrals and barn was on their right as they entered. On the left was a saloon and next to it a store. Behind the store there was a long building that looked like a bunkhouse. The station itself was a low-fronted frame building with an awning over a stretch of boardwalk, and at the hitch-rail stood a half-dozen horses. As Sartain swung down he looked at these horses. None of them had been hard ridden.

A big man lumbered out of the door, letting it slam behind him. He was followed by two more roughly dressed men and by two women, both surprisingly pretty. Across the street on the porch of the saloon a tall old man did not move, although Sartain was aware of his watching eyes.

"Hey?" The big man looked astonished. "What's happened?"

"Found him up the road, maybe six or seven miles. He'd been dry-gulched. It's Johnny Farrow."

One of the girls gave a gasp, and Kim's eyes sought her out. She was a pretty, gray-eyed girl with dark hair, much more attractive than the rather hard-looking and flamboyant blond with her. The girl stepped back against the wall, flattening her palms there, and seemed to be waiting for something. The blond's eyes fluttered to the big man who stepped down toward them.

"My name's Ollie Morse," he said. "Who are you fellows?"

"I'm Sartain." Kim was abrupt. "This is Bud Fox. We're on the drift."

No one spoke, just standing there and looking, and none of the men made the slightest move toward the body. Kim's eyes hardened as he looked them over, and then he said, "In case you're interested, the mail pouches seem all right. There was a card in his pocket said to notify Hazel Morse." Kim's eyes went to the white-faced girl who stood by the wall, biting her lip.

To his surprise it was not she but the blond who stepped forward. "I'm Hazel Morse," she said, and then turning sharply her eyes went to the two younger men. "Verne," she spoke sharply, "you an' Matty get him off that horse. Take him to the barn until you get a grave dug."

Kim Sartain felt a little flicker of feeling run through him and he glanced at Bud, who shrugged. Both men gathered up their bridle reins. "Better notify the sheriff an' the express company," Kim commented idly. "They'll probably want to know." The faint edge of sarcasm in his voice aroused the big man.

"You wouldn't be gettin' smart now, would you?" His voice was low and ugly. His gun butt was worn from much handling, and he looked as tough as he was untidy.

"Smart?" Kim Sartain shrugged. "That ain't my way, to be smart. I was just thinkin'," he added dryly, "that this young fellow sure picked a bad place to die. Nobody seems very wrought-up about it, not even the girl he wanted notified in case of death. What were you to him?" he addressed the last question to Hazel Morse suddenly.

Her face flushed angrily. "He was a friend!" she flared. "He came courtin' a few times, that was all!"

Sartain turned away and led his horse across the street to the saloon, followed by Bud Fox. Behind him there was a low murmur of voices. The older man sitting on the porch looked at them with veiled eyes. He was grizzled and dirty in a faded cotton shirt with sleeves rolled up exposing the red flannels he wore. His body was lean and the gun he had tucked in his waist-band looked used.

He got up as they went through the door into the saloon, and followed them in, moving around behind the bar. "Rye?" he questioned.

Kim nodded and watched him set out the bottle and glasses. When Kim poured a drink for Bud and himself, he replaced the bottle on the bar, and the old man stood there, looking at them. Kim tossed a silver dollar on the bar and the man made change from his pants pocket. "Any place around here a man can get a meal?" Kim asked.

"Yeah." The older man waited while Kim could have counted to fifty. "Over the road there, at the station. They serve grub. My old lady's a good cook."

"Your name Morse, too?"

"Uh huh." He scratched his stomach. "I'm Het Morse. Ollie, he runs the stage station. He's my boy. Hazel, that there blond gal you talked to, she's my gal. Verne Stecher, the young feller with the red shirt, he's my neffy, my own brother's boy. Matty Brown, he just loafs here when he ain't workin'."

Kim felt a queer little start of apprehension. He had heard of Matty Brown. The sullen youngster had killed six or seven men, one of them at Pioche only a few months back. He was known as a bad one to tangle with. Suddenly, Kim had a feeling of being hemmed in, of being surrounded by the Morse clan and their kind.

"Too bad about that express rider," Bud commented.

"Maybe," Kim suggested to Bud, "we might get us jobs ridin' the mail. With this gent dead, they might need a good man or two."

"Could be," Bud agreed. "It's worth askin' about. Who," he looked up at Het, "would we talk to? Your son?"

38

"No. Ollie, he's only the station man. You'd have to ride on over the Rubies to the Fort, or maybe down to Carson." He looked at them, his interest finally aroused. "You from around here?"

"From over the mountains," Kim said. "We been ridin' for the Tumblin' K." They had agreed not to fake a story. Their own was good enough, for neither of them had ever been connected with the law; both had always been cowhands.

"Tumblin' K?" Het nodded. "Heard of it. Gunfightin' outfit. Hear tell that McQueen feller is hell on wheels with his guns. An' that other'n, too, that youngster they call Sarten."

"Sartain," Kim said. "Emphasis on the 'tain' part."

"You know him?" Het studied Kim. "Or maybe you are him?"

"That's right." Kim did not pause to let Morse think that over, but added, "This is the slack season. No need for so many hands, an' Bud here, him an' me wanted to see some country."

"That's likely." Het indicated the darkening building across the road. "Closin' up now, until after grub. They'll fix you a bite over there. I'll let you a room upstairs, the two of you for a dollar."

Supper was a slow, silent meal. The food was good and there was lots of it, but it was heavy and the biscuits were soggy. It was far different from the cooking back on the K, as both punchers remembered regretfully. Nobody talked, for

39

eating here seemed to be a serious business.

The dark-haired girl came and went in silence, and once Kim caught her looking at him with wide, frightened eyes. He smiled a little, and a brief, trembling smile flickered on the girl's face, then was gone. Once a big woman with a face that might have been carved from red granite appeared in the door holding a large spoon. She stared at him and then went back into the kitchen. If this was Het's wife there was little of motherly love around Sand Springs.

Het chuckled suddenly, then he looked up. "You fellers got yourself a high-toned guest tonight," he said, grinning triumphantly and with some malice, too. "That dark-haired one is Kim Sartain, that gunfightin' segundo from the Tumblin' K!"

All eyes lifted, but those of Matty Brown seemed suddenly to glow with deep fire. He stared at Kim, nodding. "Heerd about yuh," he said.

"Folks talk a mighty lot," Sartain said casually. "They stretch stories pretty far."

"That's what I reckoned," Matty slapped butter on a slab of bread, his tone contemptuous.

Kim Sartain felt a little burst of anger within him and he hardened suddenly. Out of the corner of his eye he saw Bud Fox give Matty a cold, careful look. Bud was no gunslinger, but he was a fighting man and he knew trouble when he saw it. As far as that went, they sat right in the middle of plenty of trouble. Kim had guessed that right away, but he knew it with a queer excitement when he saw Ollie reach over and break a straw from the broom and start picking his teeth with it.

Outside on the porch, Fox drew closer to Sartain. "Better sleep with your gun on," he said dryly. "I don't like this setup."

"Me either. Wonder what that dark-haired girl is doin' in this den of wolves? She don't fit in, not one bit."

"We'll see," Kim said. "I think we'll stick around for awhile. When the stage goes on, we'll send a letter to Carson about jobs, but that'll be just an excuse to stay on here."

Chapter 3

Sartain kicked his feet from under the blankets in the chill of dawn. He rubbed his eyes and growled under his breath, then pulled on his wool socks and padded across the room to throw cold water on his face. When he had straightened, he looked at Bud. The lean and freckled cowhand was sleeping with his mouth open, snoring gently.

Kim grinned suddenly and looked at the bin of cold water, then remembered they would sleep here tonight and thought the better of his impulse. Crossing to the bed he sat down hard and searched under it for a boot. He pulled it on, stamping his foot into place. Bud Fox opened one wary eye. "I know, you lousy souwegian, you want me to wake up. Well, I ain't a gonna do it!" Closing his eyes he snored hard.

Sartain grinned and pulled on the other boot, then crossed to the water pitcher. Lifting it, he sloshed the water about noisily, then looked at the bed. Bud Fox had both eyes wide with alarm. "You do it," he threatened, "an' so help me, I'll kill you!"

Kim chuckled. "Get up! We got work to do!"

"Why get up? What we got to do that's so pressin'?" As he talked, Fox sat up. "When I think of eating breakfast with that outfit I get cold chills. I never did see such a low-down passel o' folks in all my days." He stretched. " 'Ceptin' for that dark-haired Jeanie."

Kim said nothing, but he was in complete agreement. As he belted on his guns he looked out the window, studying the white track of the trail. Nowhere had he seen such a misbegotten hunch of buildings or people.

"You watch that Matty Brown," Fox warned, heading for the basin. "He's pizen mean. Sticks out all over him."

"They're all of a kind, this bunch," Kim agreed. "I reckon we won't have to travel much further to find what we want. Proving it may be a full-sized job. That old man downstairs fair gives me the chills. To my notion he's the worst of the lot."

When they left the room Kim Sartain paused and glanced down the bare and empty hall. Five more doors opened off the hall, but now all were closed. There was a door at the end, too, but that must lead to the stairs he had seen from below.

Turning, they walked down the hall, their boots sounding loud in the passage. The stairs took them to the barroom where all was dark and still. The dusty bottles behind the bar, the few scattered tables with their cards and dirty glasses that stood desolate and still, all were lost in the half gloom of early day.

Outside a low wind was blowing and they hustled across to the warmth of the boardinghouse. Here a light was burning but there was no one in sight, although the table was set and they could hear sounds from the kitchen, a rattle of dishes, and then someone shaking down a stove.

Kim hung his hat on a peg and glanced into the cracked mirror on the wall. His narrow, dark face looked cold this morning. As cold as he felt. He hitched his guns to an easier place, resting his palms on the polished butts of the big .44 Russians for an instant. There were places where the checking on the walnut butt had worn almost smooth from handling.

There were hurried footsteps and then the dark-haired girl came through the door with a coffee pot. She smiled quickly, glancing from Kim to Bud and back again. "I knew it must be you. Nobody else gets around so early."

"*You* seem to," Kim said, smiling. "Are you the cook?"

"Sometimes. I usually get breakfast. Are . . . are you leaving today?"

"No." Kim watched her movements. She was a slim, lovely girl with a trim figure and a soft, charming face. "We're staying around."

For an instant she was still, listening. Then low-voiced, she said, "I wouldn't. I would ride on, quickly. Today.

Both of the cowhands watched her now. "Why?" Kim asked. "Tell us."

"I can't. But . . . but it . . . it's dangerous here. They don't like strangers stopping here. Especially now."

"What are you doing here? You don't seem to fit in."

44

She hesitated again, listening. "I have to stay. My father died owing them money. I have to work it out, and then I can go. If I tried to leave now, they would bring me back. Besides, it wouldn't be honest."

Kim Sartain looked surprised. "You think we should leave? I think *you* should leave. At once — by the next stage."

"I cannot. I . . . ," she hesitated, listening again.

Kim looked up at her. "What about Johnny Farrow? Was he in love with Hazel, and she with him?"

"He may have been, but Hazel? She loves no one but herself, unless it is Matty. I doubt even that. She would do anything for money."

She went out to the kitchen and they heard the sound of frying eggs. Kim glanced around, reached for the coffee pot, and then filled his cup. As he did so, he heard footsteps crossing the road, and then the door opened and Matty Brown came in, followed by Verne Stecher. They dropped onto the bench across the table.

Matty looked at Kim. "Up early, ain't you? Figure on pullin' out?"

"We're going to stick around. We're writin' to Carson, maybe we can get jobs ridin' with the mail or express. Sounds like it might be interesting."

"You seen Farrow. That look interesting?"

Before Kim could reply, Ollie Morse came in with his father. They looked sharply at Kim and Bud and then sat down at the table. Finishing

45

their meal, the two cowhands arose and went outside, drifting toward the stable.

"Johnny Farrow," Kim said suddenly, "started his ride ten miles west of here. He swapped horses here, and then again ten miles east, and as the next stretch was all up and down hill, rough mountain country, he finished his ride in just five miles on the third horse.

"All this route was mapped out and timed. They know those messages had to be read while in his possession, yet they couldn't have been. Nobody had time to open those pouches, open a message and then seal both of them again in the time allowed. It just couldn't be done. Unless . . ."

"Unless what?"

"Unless Johnny found a way to cut his time. All the way out here I've been studying this thing. He had to find some way to cut his time. Now he swapped horses here, an' we know that everybody here is in the one family, so to speak. We know that Johnny was sweet on Hazel. No man likes to just wave at a girl; he likes to set over coffee with her, talk a mite.

"Suppose he found a way or somebody showed him a way he could cut his time? Suppose while he sat talkin' to Hazel, these other hombres found a way to open the mail pouch?"

Bud nodded and lit his cigarette. "Yeah," he agreed, "it could have been done that way. Whatever was done, Johnny must have got wise. Then they killed him."

Chapter 4

They saddled up and, mounting their horses, started down the trail to the west. Glancing back, Kim saw Ollie Morse standing on the porch shading his eyes after them. All morning there had been an idea in the back of Kim's mind and now it came to the fore. He swung left into an arroyo and led the way swiftly in a circling movement that would bring them back to the trail east of Sand Springs.

"Where you headed for now?" Bud demanded. "You're headed right into the worst mess of mountains around here."

"Yeah," Kim slowed his pace, "but you know something? I've been drawing maps in my mind. It looks to me like that trail from Sand Springs to the next station at Burnt Rock swings somewhat wide to get around those mountains you speak of. Suppose there was a way through? Would that save time or wouldn't it?"

"Sure, if it would save distance. If there was an easy way through, why, a man might cut several miles off, and miles mean minutes."

"In other words, if a man knew a shortcut through those mountains, and he wanted to stay an' talk to his girl a while, he could do it. I've seen girls I'd take a chance like that to talk to. That Jeanie, for instance. Now she's reg'lar."

They rode on in silence for several minutes.

Before them the wall of the mountains lifted abruptly. It was not a wall, but a slope far too steep for a horse to climb and one that would have been a struggle for a mountain goat. While there were notches in the wall, none of them gave promise of an opening. As far as they could see to the north the mountains were unchanged, a series of peaks, and the wall, staggered somewhat, still.

Twice they investigated openings, but each time they ended in steep slides down which water had cascaded in wet periods. At noon they stopped, built a dry brush fire, and made coffee. But Fox ate in silence until Kim filled his cup for the third time. "Don't look good, Kim. We ain't found a thing."

"There's got to be a hole!" Kim persisted irritably. "There's no other way he could have made it."

He was wishing right now that Ward McQueen was here. The foreman of the Tumbling K had a head for problems. As for himself, well, he was some shakes in a scrap but he'd never been much for figuring angles.

Tired and dusty from travel, they returned to Sand Springs. The street between the buildings was deserted as they approached, not even a sight of Het, who apparently almost lived on the saloon stoop. They stabled their horses and rubbed them down and then started for the boardinghouse. Suddenly Kim stopped. "Bud, watch yourself! I don't like the look of this!"

Bud Fox moved right of the wide barn door, every sense alert. "What's the matter, Kim?" he whispered. "See something?"

"That's the trouble," Kim said. "I don't see anything or hear anything. It's too quiet!"

Carefully, he backed into the shadows and eased over in the darkness along the wall. It was late evening, not yet dusk, but dark when away from the wide barn door. Looking out, Kim's eye caught what was the merest suggestion of movement from a window over the saloon. Although the evening was cool, that window was open. A rifleman there could cover the barn door unseen.

Turning swiftly, Kim ran on soundless feet to the rear of the barn. Opening the door to the corral, he slid outside and scrambled over the fence, then ducked into the desert and circled until he could get across the road. All this took him no more than two minutes, but once across the road, he eased around to the back of the saloon and opened the rear door after mounting the stairs. He crept down the hall, but just as he reached for the doorknob a board creaked under his feet. He grabbed the knob and thrust the door open, hearing a faint sound from within the room as he did so.

Kim stepped into the room, gun in hand, then stopped. It was empty. On the right there was another door and he stepped swiftly to it and turned the knob. The door was locked.

There was a bed here as in his own room; there

was also chair and table, a bowl and pitcher. He stepped to the window and glanced out. There was no sound or movement anywhere. He was turning away when he heard something crunch slightly under his boot. He dropped to one knee and felt around on the floor, then picked up several twigs, broken about an inch long in each case.

Closing the door behind him, he walked along the hall and then went down the stairs. There was nobody in sight. The saloon was empty. Stepping out into the street, Sartain holstered his gun and crossed the street to the stable. "All right, Bud," he said.

As they walked to the boardinghouse he explained swiftly, then he saw a light go on inside the boardinghouse and he pushed open the door, Jeanie was just replacing the lamp chimney after lighting the lamp.

"Oh?" Was that relief in her eyes? "It's you. Did you have a nice ride?"

"So-so." He waved a hand. "Where is everybody?"

"All gone but Hazel and she's asleep. They left right after you did, only they rode the other way. They said they would be back about sundown."

Bud looked inquiringly at Kim, who shrugged his shoulders. If she was the only one around, had it been she who was in the room over the saloon? But how could she have crossed the street unseen?

Chapter 5

Several riders came up and dismounted in front of the stable and then Ollie and Matty Brown came through the door. They looked sharply at the two cowhands, but neither spoke. After a few minutes the others came in, but the meal seemed to drag on endlessly and the tension was obvious.

Yet as the meal drew to a close, Kim Sartain suddenly found himself growing more and more calm and cool. He felt a new sense of certainty and of growing confidence.

In his own mind he was positive that the killers of Johnny Farrow were here, in this room. He was also convinced that somewhere about was the stolen gold. He had both of these jobs to do: to find how the information on the shipments had been given to the outlaws, and also what had become of the gold. For the authorities were sure that thus far none of it had been sold or used.

With the new sense of certainty came something else, a knowledge that he must push these men. They were guilty and so were doubtless disturbed by the presence of the two cowhands, even though they might not suspect their purpose in being here. Kim was sure that an attempt was to have been made to kill them both that afternoon. The broken twigs were evidence enough that Farrow's killer had stood beside that window, though it could have been at some other time than today. And Ollie Morse used pieces of broom straw for toothpicks, and probably used twigs too.

"Been thinkin'," he remarked suddenly, throwing his words into the pool of silence, "about that poor youngster who was killed. I figure somebody wanted him dead mighty bad, else they would never have filled him with so much lead. Next, I get to wonderin' why he was killed."

Net Morse said nothing, sitting back in his chair and lighting his pipe. Matty continued to eat, but both Verne and Ollie were watching him. "Now I," Kim went on, "figure it must have been jealousy. Which one of you here was jealous of him seein' Hazel?"

Matty looked up sharply. "You throwin' that at me? I'm the only one livin' here who ain't related to her!"

"I figured a girl pretty as Hazel would have men comin' some distance to see her, although I did allow it might be you, Matty."

"Of course, more than one man shot Farrow," Fox contributed.

"I don't need he'p in my killin's," Matty said flatly.

Kim Sartain shrugged. "Just figurin'. Well, I reckon I'll turn in." He got to his feet. "I expect Farrow must have spent a lot of time here," he dropped the comment easily, "seein' he was sweet on Hazel."

"How could he?" Hazel demanded, getting to her feet. "He was an express rider. He only had

52

two minutes to change in, and it rarely took him that long."

"Yeah? Well, I reckoned maybe he found a way." All eyes were on Kim now. "If I was sweet on a girl, *I'd* find a way."

"Such as what?" Ollie demanded.

"Oh, maybe a shortcut through those mountains. Yeah, that would be it. Something that would give me extra time."

Matty leaned back in his chair, and suddenly he was smiling, but it was not a nice smile, Verne was staring at Sartain, his eyes murderous, Het was poker-faced, but Ollie was suddenly sweating.

"Well," Kim said, "good night all. You comin', Bud?"

Outside, Bud mopped his face. "You *crazy?* Stickin' it to 'em that way?"

A shadow moved near the window curtain and Kim heard the door open softly. "The way I figure it," he said loudly, "whoever killed that rider knew something about that gold that was stolen. I figure it must be cached around here somewhere, in the hills, maybe. It was stolen near here and whoever stole it probably didn't take it far. We better have us a look."

They crossed the street to the saloon and entered. A moment later Het came in behind them. "You fellers want a drink?" he asked genially. "Might's well have one. Makes a feller warm to go to bed on."

"Don't mind if we do," Kim replied, "an' you

have one with us."

"Sure." Het got out the bottle and glasses. He seemed to be searching for words. "Reckon," he said finally, "you know I heerd what you said about huntin' that there gold. I wouldn't, if'n I was you. Fact is, you two ain't makin' no friends around here. We uns mind our own affairs an' figure others should do likewise."

Kim grinned and lifted his glass. "Gold is anybody's business, amigo. It's yours if you find it, ours if we find it. Here's to the gold and whoever finds it, and here's to the hot place for the others!"

They tossed off their drinks and the old man filled the glasses again. "All right," he said, almost sadly. "Don't say you weren't warned. I reckon it's on your head now, but as long as you're lookin', I'll tell you. There is a shortcut."

"Yeah?" Kim Sartain's face was straight and his lips stiff.

"Uh huh. It's an old Paiute trail. Easy goin' all the way, but known to few around here. I reckon it was me put Farrow up to it. He was sweet on Hazel, so it was me told him. I aimed to he'p the boy."

"Thanks.", Kim Sartain lifted his glass to the old man. "See you tomorrow?"

Het Morse's Adam's apple bobbed and his eyes looked queer. "I reckon you will."

Upstairs in their room Sartain closed the door and propped a chair under the knob. Bud Fox threw his hat on a peg. "Now I wonder why he told us that?"

In the dim light from the lamp Kim's strongly boned face was thrown into sharp relief, his cheekbones hard and gleaming, his cheeks hollow from darkness. "You know mighty well why he told us. So we'd go there. What better place to kill snoopers than on an unknown trail where nobody but buzzards would find them?"

Bud absorbed that, his freckled face strangely pale. He pulled off a boot and rubbed his socked foot. Then he looked up. "What we goin' to do Kim?"

"Us?" Kim chuckled softly, warmly, and with real humor. "Why, Bud, you wouldn't disappoint 'em, would you? We're goin', of course!"

Chapter 6

The morning sun lay warm upon the quiet hills, and the cicadas that hummed in the greasewood seemed drowsily content. Between the knees of Kim Sartain the Appaloosa stepped out gaily, head bobbing, knees lifting, stepping as if to unheard music. And Kim Sartain sat erect in the saddle, a dark blue shirt tucked into gray wool trousers which were tucked into black, hand-tooled boots with large Mexican spurs. Kim Sartain rode coolly, and with a smile on is lips.

The mountains seemed split asunder before him, and here the sunlight fell upon the gigantic crack, the shadows lay before him, and he rode down into darkness with a hand on his thigh and a loose and ready gun inches from his hand. There was no sound, there was no movement. A mile, and the crack widened, then opened into a wide green valley across which the track of the ancient Paiute trail left a gray-white streak among the tumbled boulders and broken ledges. There was a sound of running water, and a freshness in the air, and at the fording of the stream, Kim Sartain swung down, allowing his horse to drink.

There were trees at the base of a big-as-a-house boulder, and from the shelter of these boulders stepped Matty Brown.

He stepped into the bright sunlight and stood there, and Kim Sartain saw him. And Matty

Brown took another step forward and said, speaking clearly, "I reckon that gun rep o' yours is all talk, Sartain! *Let's see!*"

His right hand slapped down fast and the gun came up smoothly and his first shot blasted harmlessly off into the vast blue sky, and then Matty turned halfway around and fell, rolling over slowly with blood staining his shirtfront and the emptiness in his eyes staring up at the emptiness in the sky, an Kim Sartain's .44 Russian lifted a little tendril of smoke toward the sky. And then Kim saw Het Morse step from the brush, with Ollie off to his right, and Verne Stecher spoke from behind him.

"Matty," Stecher said, "he allus did figure hisself faster than he was. He wanted to have his try, so we let him. Now you, snooper, we plant you here."

"Hey, where's your partner?" Ollie suddenly demanded. The big man was perspiring profusely. Only Het was quiet, negligent, almost lazy; that old man was poison wicked.

Bud's voice floated above them. "I'm right up here, Ollie. S'pose you drop your guns!"

Ollie's head jerked and fear showed on his face, stark fear. Where the voice came from he did not know, but it might have been a dozen places. Kim Sartain could feel the panic in him but his own eyes did not waver from Het's.

"Guess we better drop 'em, Pop." Ollie's voice shook. "They got us."

The old man's voice was frosty with contempt.

We're three to two. They got nothin'. Let Verne get that other'n. We'll take Sartain."

"No!" Ollie's fear was strident in his voice. The death of Matty Brown, the body lying there, had put fear all through him. "No! Don't — !"

Kim saw it coming an instant before Het squeezed off his shot, and he fired, smashing two quick ones at Het. He saw the old man jerk sharply, heard the whine of the bullet past his own head, and then he fired again, throwing himself to the right to one knee, the other leg stretched far out. Then he swung his gun to Ollie. Other guns were smashing around him, and a shot kicked dirt into his mouth and eyes. Momentarily blinded, he rolled over, lost hold on his gun and clawed at his eyes. Something tugged at his shirt and he grabbed for his left-hand gun and came up shooting. Old Het was half behind a rock and had his gun resting on it.

Kim lunged to his feet and ran directly at the old man, hearing the hard bark of a pistol and the shrill whine of a rifle bullet, and then he skidded to a halt and dropped his gun on Het. Het tried to lift his own six-shooter from the rock as Kim fired. Dust lifted from the old man's shirt and the bullet smashed him to the ground and he lost hold on his gun.

And then the shooting was past, and Kim glanced swiftly around. Bud was near the boulder where he had waited for the ambush, and Ollie was down, and Stecher was stretched at full length, hands empty.

Kim looked down at Het. The oldster's eyes were open and he was grinning. "Tough!" he whispered. "I told Matty you was tough! He wouldn't listen to . . . to an . . . to an old man . . .

"Ollie," he whispered, "no guts. If I'd o' spawned the likes o' you . . . !" His voice trailed away and he panted hoarsely.

"Het," Kim squatted beside him, "the Law sent us down here. The United States Government. That gold was rightly theirs, Het. You're goin' out, and you don't want to rob the Government, do you, Het?"

"Gover'ment?" He fumbled at the word with loose lips. He flopped his hand, trying to point at the boulder where they had waited. "Cave . . . under that boulder . . ."

His words trailed weakly away and he panted hoarsely for a few minutes, and then Kim Sartain saw a buzzard mirrored in the old man's eyes, and looking up, he saw the buzzard high overhead, and looking down, he saw that Het Morse was dead.

Bud Fox walked up slowly, his freckles showing against the gray of his face. "Never liked this killin' business," he said. "I ain't got the stomach for it." He looked up at Kim. "Reckon you pegged it right when you had me come on ahead."

"An' you picked the right spot to wait," Kim agreed dryly.

"It was the only one, actually." Bud Fox looked around. "Reckon we can load that gold on their horses. You goin' to stop by for that Jeanie girl?"

"Why, sure!" Kim whistled and watched the Appaloosa come toward him. "We'll take her to Carson. I reckon any debt she owed has been liquidated right here." Then he said soberly, "I was sure the first day we rode in. Behind the bottles on the back bar I saw an awl an' a leather-worker's needle. They opened the stitching on those pouches while Farrow was sparkin' Hazel. They got the information thataway, then put the letters back and stitched 'em up again."

Behind them they left three mounds of earth and a cross marking the grave of Het Morse. "He was a tough old man," Bud Fox said gloomily.

Kim Sartain looked at the trail ahead where the sunlight lay. A cicada lifted its thin whine from the brush along the trail. Kim removed his hat and mopped his brow. "He sure was," he said.

THAT
TRIGGERNOMETRY
TENDERFOOT

It was shortly after daybreak when the stage from Cottonwood rolled to a stop before the wide veranda of the Ewing Ranch house. Jim Carey hauled back on the lines to stop the dusty, champing horses. Taking a turn around the brake handle, he climbed down from the seat.

A grin twisted his lips under the brushy mustache as he went up the steps. He pulled open the door and thrust his head inside. "Hey, Frank!" he yelled. "Yuh t' home?"

"Sure thing!" A deep voice boomed in the hallway. "Come on back here, Jim!"

Jim Carey hitched his six-shooter to a more comfortable position and strode back to the long room where Frank Ewing sat at the breakfast table.

"I brung the new schoolma'am out," he said slowly, his eyes gleaming with ironic humor as the heads of the cowhands came up, and their eyes brightened with interest.

"Good thing!" Ewing bellowed. His softest tone could be heard over twenty acres. "The boys are rarin' t' see her! So's Claire! I reckon we can bed her down with Claire so's they can talk all they're a mind to!"

Jim Carey picked up the coffee cup Ma Ewing placed for him. "Don't reckon yuh will, Frank," he said. "Wouldn't be quite fittin'."

"What?" Ewing rared back in his chair. "Yuh mean this here Boston female is so high an' mighty she figgers she's too good for my daughter? Why . . . !"

"It ain't thet," Jim's grin spread all over his red face, "on'y the new schoolma'am ain't a she, she's a he!"

"What?"

Frank Ewing's bellow caused deer to lift their startled heads in the brakes of the Rampart, ten miles away. The cowhands stiffened, their faces stricken with disappointment and horror, a horror that stemmed from the realization that anything wearing pants could actually teach school.

"Sure thing!" Jim was chuckling now. "She's a he! He's waitin' outside now!"

"Well!" Ma Ewing put her hands on her wide hips, "yuh took long enough t' tell us! Fetch the pore critter in! Don't leave him standin' out there by hisself!"

Carey got up, still chuckling at the stupefied expressions on the faces of the cowhands and walked to the door. "Hey, you! Come on in an' set for chuck! Reckon," he added, glancing around, "I'll be rollin'. No time t' dally."

He hesitated, grinning. "Reckon yuh boys'll be right gentle with him. He's plumb new t' the West! Wanted t' git off and pet one o' them ornery longhorns up the pass!"

Stretch Magoon's long, homely face was bland with innocence. "Wal, now! I calls that right touchin'! I reckon we'll have t' give him a chance

64

t' pat ol' Humpy!"

The cowhands broke into a chuckle and even Claire found herself smiling at the idea. Then, at the approaching footsteps in the hall they all looked up expectantly.

The new schoolma'am stepped shyly into the door carrying a carpetbag in one hand, a hard black hat in the other.

He wore a black suit, stiff with newness, and a high white collar. His hair was dark and wavy, his eyes blue and without guile. His face was pink and white with a scattering of freckles over the nose.

He was smiling now, and there was something boyish and friendly about him. Claire sat up a little straighter, stirred by a new and perplexing curiosity.

"Come in an' set," Ma Ewing declared heartily. "You're jest in time for breakfast!"

"My name's Vance Brady," he suggested. "They call me Van."

"Mine's Ewing," the big cattleman replied. "This here's my wife, an' thet's my daughter, Claire. She's been teachin' the young uns, but they's a passel o' big uns, too big for her t' handle."

He glanced at Brady. "An' some o' them's purty durned big, an' plenty ornery!"

"That's fine!" Brady said seriously. "There is nothing like the bright energy of youth."

Stretch Magoon's long, melancholy face lifted. "Thet sure touches me," he said solemnly, "thet

65

bright energy of youth. I'm Stretch Magoon," he added, "an' we'll do all we kin t' make yor stay onforgettable!"

Ma Ewing frowned at Magoon, and he averted his eyes and looked sadly down at his plate.

"Reckon yuh come a fur piece," Ewing suggested, chewing on a broom straw. "From Boston, ain't yuh?"

"Near Boston," Brady replied, smiling. "Is the school close by?"

"Down the road about ten mile," Ewing replied, "jest beyond the old Shanahan place."

Brady glanced up. "The Shanahan place? Is that a farm? I mean . . . a ranch? Maybe I could live there, a little closer to my work?"

Ewing shook his leonine head and tugged at his yellow mustache. "Nobody lives there. Old Mike Shanahan was killed nigh on a year back. If none of his relatives come t' live on the place afore thet year is up, then it's open t' anybody who will claim it an' hold it."

"It was a damn' fool idea!" Curly Ward said. He was a big, blond puncher, handsome in a strong, masculine way. "Old Mike should of knowed it was jest an invitation for Pete Ritter t' move in! With his gunfightin' cowhands an' the money he's ready t' spend, nobody around here can buck him. He's got more'n he needs now."

"Wal," Stretch said positively, "he's sure goin' t' have thet place! The will done said if'n any of his relatives showed up they'd have t' live on the place thirty days o' this year t' claim it!"

"It would appear," Van Brady said, "that my staying there would be impractical. From what you say I doubt if Mr. Ritter would allow it."

Ward grinned, faint humor in his eyes. "He sure wouldn't! Not even a *he* schoolma'am!" The contempt in his voice was undisguised.

Claire's face flushed with embarrassment for the teacher, and Brady looked up. "I take it you are unaccustomed to male teachers," he said politely. "There are many in the East. I believe this would be a good country for some of them."

He looked over at Ewing. "Have you a conveyance? A horse or something that would get me down to my school? I'd like to look it over."

"Now ain't thet pecoolyar!" Magoon looked up, a warm smile illuminating his face. "I was jest thinkin' yuh'd be wantin' a hoss! We got a yaller hoss out here I'm sure would be jest the thing for yuh!"

Claire sat bolt upright and she started to speak, but before she could utter her protest, Van Brady smiled. "Why, how nice, Mr. Magoon! Thank you very much!"

When Brady followed Magoon from the room Claire started to her feet. "Father!" she protested. "Are you going to let them put that boy on that buckskin devil?"

"Now, Claire, don't fret yourself!" Ewing said, grinning. "He won't do no such thing! Buck will toss him afore he gits settled in the saddle! The fall won't hurt him none. Let the boys git it out of their system. Besides," he added glumly, "I ain't so sure I like no he schoolma'am m'self!"

Claire Ewing got to her feet and started for the door, the others trooping expectantly behind.

Magoon already had a saddle on the lazy-looking buckskin, and was cinching it tight, plenty tight, and talking to Brady. Curly Ward was standing nearby, lighting a smoke and grinning with anticipation. Web Fancher and the other hands gathered around, striving to look innocent.

"He's a right nice hoss," Stretch said sorrowfully, "a gentle hoss. I reckon the boss might let yuh ride him all the time."

"Better put on these spurs," he added. "He's kind o' lazy an' won't really git goin' less yuh nudge him right sharp."

Van Brady sat down and fumbled with the spurs until Stretch knelt beside him and helped put them on. Then Van got up. The yellow horse looked around, speculative curiosity on his face, a face almost as sad and woebegone as Magoon's.

Brady put a tentative foot in the stirrup, then swung his leg over the buckskin. Stretch Magoon stepped back warily, putting distance between himself and the horse. "Yuh'll have t' gouge him purty stiff," he called. "He's sho nuff lazy!"

Van Brady touched the yellow horse with the spurs, then at no movement, he jerked his heels out and jammed both spurs into the buckskin's flanks.

The buckskin exploded like a ton of dynamite. With one catlike leap, he sprang forward and dug in his forefeet. The he schoolma'am shot forward, but somehow barely missed losing his seat, then the yellow horse swapped ends three times so fast he was merely a blur of movement, and then he began to buck like a fiend out of hell.

Brady lost a stirrup, and swung clear around until he was facing the buckskin's rear, clawing madly for the saddle horn. But when the horse swapped ends again, he miraculously flopped back into the saddle. Three times the buckskin sunfished madly, and then went across the ranch yard swapping ends and buck jumping until every bone in Brady's body was wracked. Yet somehow the he schoolma'am held on.

Then the equine cyclone went completely berserk. He leaped wildly toward the morning clouds, then charged for the corral fence, but just as he swung broadside to it the schoolma'am lost a stirrup! His hard hat was gone, his coat tails flying in the wind, but he was still aboard.

As suddenly as it had begun, the yellow horse stopped bucking and trotted toward the ranch house, Brady pulled him to a halt, and the buckskin stood, trembling in every limb.

Stretch Magoon's face was a blank study, and Curly Ward was staring, half angry.

Van Brady smiled and wiped the perspiration from his brow with a white handkerchief. "He is spirited, isn't he?" he said innocently. Then he glanced at Stretch Magoon. "Would you hand me my hat? I'm afraid he bucked it off!"

Walking as if in a trance, his solemn eyes even

more owllike than before, Magoon went over and picked up the hard hat. Almost subconsciously, he brushed off the dust, then handed it to Brady.

The he schoolma'am smiled. "You've been very kind," he said. "I don't know what I'd have done if I got one of those really excitable horses you cowmen ride!" He looked at Ewing. "Which way do I go to the school?"

"That road right ahead," Ewing said. "Foller past them cottonwoods an' cross the crick when you come t' the willows. That's where you'll see the old Shanahan place. The schoolhouse is a might further on."

Curly Ward stared after him. "Did you see that?" he demanded. "Talk about a fool for luck! That pilgrim was almost off four, five times, an' then bucked right back into the saddle! If I hadn't seen it I wouldn't believe it! He was all over that hoss like a cork in a mill stream! How he stuck with him is more'n I can guess!"

Claire's eyes were narrow as she stared after the teacher. The light in them was faintly curious. "I'm not so sure!" she said softly. "I'm not so sure!"

Van Brady rode straight, sitting stiffly erect in the saddle until he was over the crest of the hill. Then he glanced around, safely out of sight of the ranch house, and out of hearing he exploded into laughter. He roared and laughed and finally settled into chuckling. "That Magoon!" he said to the yellow horse. "I won't forget that long horse face of his if I live to be a hundred! He

70

stood there with his mouth open like the end of a tunnel!"

He patted the yellow horse on the shoulder. "You sure can buck, you yellow hunk of misery!" he said, grinning. "I was afraid I was overplaying my hand!"

" 'You'll have t' gouge him pretty stiff,' Magoon says," Van repeated, chuckling. "Why, that long-faced baboon probably never saw the day he could ride this sinful old coyote bait!"

The old Shanahan place was a cluster of buildings gathered in a hollow of the hills not far from Willow Creek. Van Brady glanced at them curiously, but did not stop. When he had skirted the hill he rode down the slight grade to the log school, built on a pleasant little flat not far from the creek.

For an hour he scouted around, getting the lay of the land. Twice, back in the willow grove, he dismounted and dug in the soil. Each time he carefully covered the spot with sod and then with dry grass.

Not over two miles away Web Fancher was sitting among the junipers on the hillside, talking to burly Neil Pratt, foreman for Pete Ritter. "He ain't nobody," Web said, disgustedly, "jest a he schoolma'am from back Boston way. He's the on'y stranger that's been around.

"Hell!" he exploded. "Why don't Pete move in an' take over the place instead o' all this pussyfootin' around? Ever'body 'lows he kin do it!"

71

Pratt shrugged. "He's pretty shrewd. Knows what he's doin' most always. If'n anybody makes a pass at movin' in over here, you get word t' me right fast!"

In her room at the ranch, Claire was writing a letter to Spanish John Roderigo, a rodeo and circus hand who had once worked for the ranch. She ended the brief note with a concise paragraph.

What I want is the name, and description if possible, of the man who did the clown riding act with the Carson Shows two years ago. You will remember, you took me to that show when I was attending school.

"We'll just see, Mr. Schoolteacher Brady!" she said to herself. "I've a few ideas of my own!"

Sunday morning was the time Magoon rode in for the mail. He saddled his horse, then went up to the kitchen. When he returned, he swung into the saddle.

Instantly, the paint exploded into a squealing fury of bucking. Caught entirely by surprise, for the paint hadn't humped his back in weeks, Magoon hit the ground and rolled over in a cloud of dust while the paint went buck jumping away across the ranch yard.

Nearly everyone had been outside, and Stretch heaved his six feet five from the dust with a pained expression on his face. The eight or nine cowhands were roaring with laughter.

The schoolma'am shook his head sadly. He walked over and picked up Magoon's sombrero, dusted it carefully, and handed it to him. "He *is* spirited, isn't he?"

"Now what do you s'pose got into that mangy crow bait?" Magoon demanded. "He ain't bucked in a long time . . . hey?" He stopped, glaring at Curly. "You ain't been up t' no monkey business?"

"Me?" Curly was honestly startled. "Not a bit of it!"

Stretch limped after the paint and led it up to the corral once more. Then, feeling under the loosened saddle, he found the cockleburr. He glared at Curly Ward. "Why, you ornery, cow rastlin' horny toad, I got a notion t' —"

"Better get that mail," Claire said. "You can settle it later."

Still growling, Magoon started for town. Claire turned and looked at Van Brady. He wiped the grin from his face. "Ever hear of that little cowboy prank Mr. Brady?" she asked sweetly. "Putting a burr under a man's saddle?"

"Is that what happened?" he asked innocently. "I thought his horse was just a little excited."

When he turned away, she looked after him. Her father walked up and put his hand on her shoulder. "What's the matter, Claire? You look like you had somethin' on your mind. Ain't fallin' for that he schoolma'am are you?"

"No," she said sharply, "I'm not! And between us, I'm not so sure he's a teacher!"

The next day she kept her ears tuned to what was happening in the other room of the two-room school. Not only was Van Brady teaching, but he had even the bigger boys interested. He was making the fight at Lexington and Concord so interesting that Claire overheard the boys discussing it when they rode toward home.

"You know," he said to her as they started toward the ranch. "I am going to miss these rides, but I believe I could do some things around the school that need doing if I stayed right here at the school. Anyway, I always wanted to camp out a little."

"You mean, you're going to move up here? Camp out?" she was incredulous.

"Yes, I am. Right over there in the willows by the stream. I think I'd like it."

The following day he moved his gear into the willows and set up camp. Van Brady scratched his head thoughtfully. "This is going to be tough," he told the buckskin. "How am I going to make that camp comfortable without letting them know I'm no greenhorn?"

Web Fancher rode over to the Circle R. "That new schoolteacher's done moved over t' the school," he said. "Didn't know if it mattered none."

"The school?" Pratt shook his head. "Just so's he don't take no fool notion t' move over to the Shanahan place."

The first class was in session the following

74

morning when there was a clatter of horse's
hooves outside and the door was suddenly flung
open. Neil Pratt strode into the room, slapping
his thigh with a quirt. "You!" he pointed with
the quirt at Tom Mawson, the nester's son.
"Ain't I told you t' stay off'n the Circle R? You
come here! I'm goin' t' learn you a thing or two!"

He grabbed Tom's shoulder and jerked him
from the seat. The next instant, a hand seized
him by the belt, and he was jerked bodily from
the floor and slammed back into the wall. Before
he could realize what had happened, Van Brady
was standing in front of him.

"Listen, you!" Brady snapped. "You keep your
hands off these kids! And don't come barging
into one of my classes when it's in session. Understand?"

Pratt heaved himself erect, his face suffused
with rage. "Why, you . . . !" His fist started, but
almost as soon as it started, something smashed
his lips back into his teeth and he hit the door,
tumbling to the ground outside.

He scrambled to his feet with an inarticulate
growl of frury. Claire, her face white, saw Neil
Pratt hurl himself at Brady.

The Circle R foreman was a notorious brawler,
a huge man weighing over two hundred. Brady
could never have weighed more than one hundred and fifty. Slim, wiry, but with broad shoulders, Brady looked much smaller than the Circle
R foreman.

Neil Pratt, blood trickling from his smashed

lips, stared at Brady. "Why, you white-livered baby!" he sneered. "I'll beat you t' a pulp!"

Four Circle R riders sat their horses, watching with interest. Pratt walked in, his face ugly. Coolly, Van Brady waited for him. A cowhand from boyhood, he had been places and learned other things. Pratt lunged, but his right missed, and Brady stepped inside, smashing two wicked blows to the body, then whipping a right hook to Pratt's cheek that cut to the bone.

Furious, Pratt tried to grab him. Van Brady was smooth, easy on his feet, his lips set, he glided in and out, boxing coolly, battering Pratt with punch after punch. Claire, astonished, suddenly realized what an incredible thing was happening. The schoolteacher was whipping Pratt!

Pratt caught Brady with a right swing and knocked him against the 'dobe wall of the school; when he lunged after him, Brady's foot caught him in the chest and shoved him back. Then, before he could get set, Van Brady moved in, smashed a left jab into his teeth, and crossed a chopping right to the chin. Pratt ducked his head and charged, but Brady was out of the way, and a snapping left bit into Pratt's ear, making his head ring.

He whirled, glaring wildly, and Brady moved in, feinted Pratt into a right swing, and then smashed a right to the body. Pratt tried again and took a left and a right. Brady wasn't moving away now, he was weaving inside of Pratt's vicious punches and nailing the big foreman with blow after blow in the stomach.

Pratt's breath was coming heavily now. The cut on his cheekbone was staining his shirt with blood, his lips were pulpy, his ear swollen. He ducked his head and started in, but two fast left jabs cut his eyebrow, and a right smashed his nose.

With an oath, Lefty Brooks, one of the Circle R hands, dropped from his horse and started forward. "Hold it!" Stretch Magoon stepped around the corner of the school. "Jest set still an' watch this," he said grimly. "You all reckoned Pratt was some shakes of a fighter. Wal, watch a man fifty pounds lighter beat his thick head in!"

Neil Pratt wiped the blood from his face with the back of his hand; he was swaying on his feet. Somehow, something was wrong. In all his fights his huge fists or his great strength had won quickly. Here was a man who didn't run away, who was always in there close, cutting, stabbing, slicing him with knifing punches, yet he couldn't hit him!

Pratt spread his hands, trying to get close. Suddenly Brady's shoulder was invitingly close. He lunged to grab it, but somehow Brady caught his wrist, bent suddenly, and Pratt found himself flying through the air to land heavily on the turf a half-dozen feet away.

Van Brady was breathing easily, and he was smiling now. "Get up, Big Boy!" he said softly. "I want to show you what happens to men who bust into my classes!"

Pratt heaved himself heavily to his feet. Brady did not wait. He walked up to him, and hooked both hands hard to the head. Pratt started to fall, and Brady caught him by the hair and smashed him in the face with three wicked uppercuts. Then he let go and shoved, and Pratt toppled over on the ground.

"Take him," Brady said to the Ritter hands, "take him home. He'll need a good rest!"

Sullenly, the Ritter hands helped Pratt to a horse and started off. Van Brady turned, wiping the sweat from his face. His clothes were not mussed, not even his wavy hair. The children stood staring admiringly as he walked to the pump to wash his bloody fists.

"You did a job," Magoon said solemnly. "I never seen a man fight like that. He couldn't hit you."

"They call it boxing," Van said, straightening up. "Fighting is just like punching cows or trapping fur. It has to be learned. It isn't anything fancy, it is just a lot of tricks learned over many years by a lot of different men, each one a good fighter. When you know a lot of them you become a skillful boxer."

He looked up at Stretch. "Thanks," he said, "for keeping that monkey off my back."

"It won't be enough, though," Magoon said. You got t' get a gun. They'll be back. That Pratt is mean!"

The Circle R was standing around staring as

Neil Pratt was helped from his horse. Both eyes were swollen tight shut. His face was a scarred and bloody mass.

"What happened?" Ritter demanded.

He was a tight-faced, hard-mouthed man with mean eyes. Some said he was a killer. That he had twenty killings behind him. He always wore two guns.

"That schoolteacher," Brooks said, "the one that's livin' at the schoolhouse."

Pete Ritter stepped down from the porch, his face livid. "Livin' at the schoolhouse?" he snapped. "Don't you know that's on the Shanahan place? Jest loaned for a school? You pack o' flea-brained dolts, that hombre may be a Shanahan!"

In her own room, Claire Ewing was reading a letter from Spanish John.

That hombre wot done the clown trik ridin ack was Shanahan Brady. He cum from Montana somewheres, but his pappy cum from Arizony, like us. He was a plumb salty hombre. For moren a year he was a prizefighter in Noo Yawk, an he done trick shootin in the show, too. If'n he's out thar, yuh tell the boys to lay off. He ain't no pilgrum.

The table was crowded when she walked in with the letter in her hands. Coolly, she read it.

"Why, that ornery coyote!" Magoon declared. "He done that ridin' ack afore! I got a good notion t' beat his . . ." The memory of Neil

79

Pratt's face came back to him. "No," he finished, "I guess I better not."

"How'd you guess?" Ewing asked her.

"That riding. I saw him do it on a circus, back East, when I was in school. He was supposed to be a clown, nearly got bucked off all the time, but always stayed on."

"Ritter'll guess," Magoon said. "He'll run him off."

Web Fancher shoved back from the table. He got up. "I ain't hongry," he said, and disappeared through the door. A moment later there was a clatter of horse's hooves.

"Goin' t' warn Ritter. I wondered what that coyote was up to!" Ward said. He got up. "Well, ain't speakin' for nobody but myself but I'm sidin' the teacher!"

In the camp among the willows, Shan Brady was digging into his war bag. He had little time, he knew. Ritter would hear of this, and from all he had learned the Circle R boss would be smart enough to put two and two together. Besides, he might know that Old Mike had allowed the school to be built on his place.

They would come for him, and he wanted to be ready. He had never killed a man, and he didn't want to now. There were four, no, that Mexican in Sonora made five, who had tried to kill him. Each of them had lived through it, but each time they had collected a bullet in the hand or arm.

Digging deeper in the war bag he drew out twin cartridge belts and two heavy Colt .45's in black, silver-mounted holsters. The belt and holsters were rodeo, showman's gear. The guns were strictly business, and looked it.

With those guns he had shot cigarettes from men's mouths, shot buttons from their coats.

Rolling up a fresh smoke, he studied the situation. His position had not been chosen only for camping facilities, and not only because it was on the Shanahan place. It had been chosen for defense, as well.

Logs had rolled downstream during flood seasons, and he had found several of them in an excellent position. He had dragged more down close, and under the pretext of gathering wood, he had built several traps at strategic places. Now, working fast, he dragged up more logs and rolled them into place. The stream provided him with water, and he had plenty of grub. He had seen to that.

They had laughed at him for that, behind his back. "That teacher must think he's goin' t' feed an army!" they had said. But he was planning, laying in a supply of food.

His position was nicely chosen. From three sides he could see anyone who approached. The willows and the log wall gave him some concealment as well as cover.

It was an hour after daylight when he saw them coming, Pete Ritter himself in the lead. Behind him were six men, riding in a tight knot. When they were thirty yards away, he lifted his rifle and spoke, "Keep back, Ritter! I don't want any trouble from you!"

"You got trouble!" Ritter shouted angrily. "You get off that place, an' get out of the country!"

"I'm Shanahan Brady!" Shan yelled, "an' I'm stayin'! Come any closer, an' somebody gets hurt!"

"Let's go!" Ritter snarled angrily. "We'll run the durned fool clear over the border!"

He started forward. Shan threw down on him and fired four fast shots. They were timed, quick and accurate. The first shot dropped a horse, the second picked the hat from Ritter's head, taking a lock of hair with it, the third burned Lefty Brooks's gun hand, and he dropped his six-shooter and grabbed the hand to him with a curse of rage. The fourth shot took the lobe from a man's ear.

The attack broke and the riders turned and raced for shelter. Shan fired two more shots after them, dusting their heels.

Calmly, he reloaded. "That was the beginning," he said. "Now we'll get the real thing."

Chewing on a biscuit, he waited. Suddenly, he glanced at the biscuit. "That Claire girl," he said, "can cook, too! Who'd a thought it?"

The morning wore on. Several times, he sized up the rocky slope behind him. That was the danger point. Yet he had built his log wall higher there, and he had a plan.

Suddenly, rifles began to pop and shots were dusting the logs around him. He waited. Then he glimpsed, four hundred yards away, what seemed to be a man's leg. He fired, and heard a yell of pain.

Suddenly, a shot rang out from behind him and a bullet thudded into the log within an inch of his head. Hurriedly, he rolled over into the shelter of the log wall. No sooner there than getting to his knees he crawled into the willows away from camp, then slid into the streambed.

Rising behind the shelter of the banks, he ran swiftly upstream. Rounding a bend, he crawled up behind some boulders, then drifted along the slope. Panting, he dropped into place behind a granite boulder and peered around the edge.

A man he recognized as one of those who had come to the school with Pratt was lying thirty yards away, rifle in hand. Shan fired instantly, burning the sniper's ribs with a bullet. The man let out a yell of alarm and scrambled to his feet and started to run.

Lying still, Shan hazed the fellow downhill, cutting his clothes to ribbons, twice knocking him down with shots at his heels.

"All right!" The voice was cold, triumphant. "The fun's over! Git up!"

Turning, he saw Pete Ritter standing behind him, gun in hand. With him were Lefty Brooks and a man Brady recognized as Web Fancher from the Ewing ranch. "I figgered you might use that crickbed!" Pete sneered. "Figgered I might use it my ownself. Now we got you. Fust, you go back t' the ranch an' we let Neil get his evens with you. Then you start for the state line. . . . You never get there!"

It was now or never. Shan Brady knew that instantly. Once they got their hands on him he was through. Ritter had him covered, but . . . his hands were a blur as they swept down for the guns.

Somebody yelled, and he saw Pete's eyes blazing behind a red-mouthed gun. Something hit him in the shoulder, and he shot, and even as he triggered his first six-gun, he realized that what he had always feared was not happening . . . he was not losing his head!

Coolly as though on exhibition, he was shooting. Ritter wavered in front of him, and suddenly he saw other Circle R riders appearing, and there seemed to be a roaring of guns behind him. Gunsmoke filled the air.

Fancher was down on his hands and knees, a pool of blood forming under him; Ritter was gone; and Lefty Brooks was backing up, his shirt turning dark, his face pale.

Then, suddenly as it began, it was over. He stepped back, and then a hand dropped on his shoulder. He turned. It was Magoon.

"Some shootin'!" Magoon said, grinning. Curly Ward and big Frank Ewing were also closing in, all with ready guns. "You took Ritter an' Brooks out of there! I got Fancher! That yeller belly of a traitor! Eatin' our grub an' working for Ritter!"

Claire rode up the slope, her hair blowing in the wind. She carried a rifle. He looked up at her. "You, too? I didn't know women ever fought in this man's country?"

"They do when their men — !" Her face flushed. "I mean they do when their schools are in danger! After all, you're our best teacher in years!"

He turned and started down the slope with her. "Reckon that old Shanahan place could be fixed up?" he asked. "I think it'd be a good place t' have the teachers live, don't you? It could be mighty liveable."

"Why, yes, but . . . ," she stopped.

"Oh, we'd get a preacher down from Hurston!" he said, grinning. "That would make it all sort of legal, and everything. Of course," he added, remembering the biscuits, "you'd have to find time to cook, too!"

She flushed. Then laughed. "For you, I think I could!"

Shan Brady looked down at the house Old Mike had built. It was a nice house. It was a very nice house. With some curtains in the window, and the smell of cooking. . . .

THE TOWN
NO GUNS COULD
TAME

Chapter 1
Town Tamer
Wanted!

The miner called Perry stepped from the bucket and leaned his pick and shovel against a boulder. He was a big man with broad shoulders and narrow hips. Despite the wet, clinging diggin' clothes, he moved with the ease and freedom of a big cat. His greenish eyes turned toward Doc Greenley, banker, postmaster, and saloon man of Basin City, who was talking with the other townsmen.

Perry's head and arms were bare, and the woolen undershirt failed to cover the mighty muscles that rippled along his back and shoulders. One of the men, noting the powerful arms and the strong neck, turned and said something to the others. They nodded, together.

"Hey, Perry," Doc Greenley called, "drift over here, will you? Me and these two gents want to make a proposition to you."

Casually, Perry picked up the spare pick handle leaning against the boulder and walked over, his wet clothes sloshing as he moved. He stopped when he reached the trio, and his eyes studied them, coldly penetrating. The three men shifted uneasily.

"Go ahead with it, then," Perry said shortly.

"It's like this," Doc explained. "Buff McCarty" — he nodded toward the larger of his two companions — "and Wade Manning, here, and myself have been worried about the rough element from the mines. They seem to be taking over the town. No respectable citizen or their womenfolks are safe. And as for the hold-ups that have been raising hell with us businessmen. . . ." Doc Greenley mopped his brow with a fresh bandanna handkerchief, letting the sentence go unfinished.

"We want you to help us, Perry," the heavy-set, honest-faced McCarty put in. "Manning, here, runs the freight line and I have the general supply outfit. We're all substantial citizens and need a man of your type for town marshal."

"As soon as I heard you were here, I told the boys you were just the man for us," Greenley put in eagerly.

Perry's green eyes narrowed thoughtfully. "I see." His gaze shifted from Doc Greenley, the most prominent and wealthiest man there, to the stolid McCarty, and then to the young townsman, Wade Manning. He smiled a little. "The town fathers, out in force, eh?" He glanced at Wade, looking at him thoughtfully. "But where's Rafe Landon, owner of the Sluice Box Bar?"

"Rafe Landon?" Doc Greenley's eyes glinted. "Why, his bar is the hangout for this tough crowd! In fact, we have reason to suspect —"

"Better let Perry form his own suspicions, Doc," wade Manning interrupted. "I'm not at

90

all sure about Rafe."

"You may not be," Greenley snapped, "but I am! Perry, I'm convinced that Landon is the ringleader of the whole kit an' caboodle of the killers and renegades we're trying to clean out!"

"Why," Perry said suddenly, "do you choose this particular time to pick a marshal? There must be a reason."

"There is," Wade Manning agreed. "You probably know about the volume of gold production here. Anyway, Doc has better than two hundred thousand in his big vault now. I have about half that much. There's a rumor around of a plot to loot the stage of the whole load."

"It's Landon," Greenley said, "that's who it is! An' do you know what *I* think?" He looked from one to the other, pulling excitedly at his ear lobe. "I think Rafe Landon is none other than *Clip Haynes,* the toughest, coldest gunman who ever pulled a trigger!"

Perry's eyes narrowed. "I heard he was down in Arizona."

"But I happen to know," Greenley said sharply, "that Clip Haynes headed this way — with the ten thousand he got from that stage job near Goldroad!"

Perry looked at Doc thoughtfully. "Maybe so. It could be that way, all right." He glanced at Buff McCarty, who was watching him from his small blue eyes. "Sure, I'll take the job! I'll ride in tonight, by the canyon trail."

The three men walked to their horses, and

91

Perry turned abruptly back to the mine office to draw his time.

The moon was rising when the man called Perry swung onto his horse and took the canyon trail for Basin City. The big black stepped out swiftly, and the man lounged in the saddle, his eyes narrowed with thought. He rode with the ease of one long accustomed to the saddle, and almost without thinking kept to the shadows along the road, guiding his horse neatly so as to render it almost invisible in the dim light.

From the black, flat-crowned hat tied under his chin with a rawhide thong to the hand-tooled cowman's boots, his costume offered nothing that would catch the glint of light or prevent him from merging indistinguishably with his background. Even the two big guns with their polished wooden butts, tied down and ready for use, harmonized perfectly with his somber dress.

The trail dipped through canyons and wound around lofty mesas, and once he forded a small stream. Shortly after, riding through a maze of gigantic boulders, he reined in sharply. His keen ear had detected a sudden sound.

Even as he came to a halt he heard the hard rattle of hooves from a running horse somewhere on the trail ahead, and almost at the same instant, the sharp *spang* of a high-powered rifle.

Soundlessly, he slid from the saddle, and even before his feet touched the sand of the trail, his guns were gripped in his big hands. Tensely, he ran forward, staying in the soft sand where his feet made no noise. Suddenly, dead ahead of him and just around a huge boulder, a pistol roared. He jerked to a halt, and eased around the rock.

A black figure of a man was on its knees in the road. Just as the man looked around, the rifle up on the mountainside crashed again, and the kneeling figure spilled over on its face.

Perry's gun roared at the flash of the rifle, and roared again as a bullet whipped by his ear. The rifle fired once more, and Perry felt his hat jerk on his head as he emptied his gun at the concealed marksman.

There was no reply. Cautiously Perry lifted his head, then began to inch toward the dark figure sprawled in the road before him. A match flared suddenly up on the hillside, and Perry started to fire, then held it. The man might think him dead, and his present position was too open to take a chance. As he reached the body, the rattle of a horse's hooves faded rapidly into the distance.

Perry's lips set grimly. Then he got to his knees and lifted the body.

It was a boy — an attractive, fair-haired youngster. He had been shot twice, once through the body, and once through the head. Perry started to rise.

"Hold it!" The voice was that of a woman, but it was cold and even. "One move and I'll shoot!"

She was standing at one side of the road with

a pistol aimed at Perry's belt line. Even in the moonlight she was lovely. Perry held perfectly still, riveted to the position as much by her beauty as by the gun she held so steadily.

"You murderer!" she said, her voice low with contempt. "Stand up, and keep your hands high!"

He put the boy gently back on the ground and got to his feet. "I'm afraid you're mistaken, miss," he said. "I didn't kill this boy."

"Don't make yourself a liar as well as a killer!" she exclaimed. "Didn't I hear you shooting? Haven't I eyes?"

"While you're holding me here," he said gently, "the real killer is making his getaway. If you'll put down that gun, I'll explain."

"Explain?" There was just a hint of hysteria in her voice. "After you've killed my brother?"

"Your brother?" he was startled now. "Why, I didn't —"

Her voice trembled, but the gun was unrelenting. "You didn't know, I suppose, that you killed Wade Manning?" Her disbelief was evident in her tone.

"Wade Manning?" he stepped forward. "Why, this isn't Wade Manning!"

"Not — not Wade?" her voice was incredulous. "But who is it then?"

He stepped back. "Take a look, Miss Manning. I don't know many people around here. I met your brother today at the Indian Creek Diggin's. He's a sight older than this poor youngster."

94

She dropped to her knees beside the boy. Then she looked up. "Why, this is young Tommy McCarty! What in the world can he be doing out here tonight?"

"Any relation to Buff McCarty?" he asked quickly.

"His son." Her eyes misted with tears. "Oh, this is awful! We — we came over the trail from Salt Lake together, his folks and mine!"

He took her by the shoulders. "Listen, Miss Manning. I don't like to butt in, you knowin' the lad an' all, but your brother came out here to see me today. He wanted me to be marshal here in Basin City. I took the job, so I guess this is the first part right here."

She drew back, aghast. "Then you — you're *Clip Haynes!*"

It was his turn to be startled now. "Who told you that?" he demanded. Things were moving a little too fast. "Who knew I was Clip Haynes?"

"Wade. He recognized you today. The others don't now. He wanted to see you tonight about something. He said it would take a man like you to handle the law job here."

Frowning thoughtfully, he caught up the boy's horse, grazing nearby, and lashed the body to the saddle. Then he mounted the big black, and the girl swung up on her pinto. Silently they took the trail for Basin City.

Despite the fact that she seemed to have accepted him, he could sense the suspicion that held her aloof. The fact remained that she had found him kneeling over the body, six-gun in hand. He could scarcely blame her. After all, he was not a simple miner named Perry. He was Clip Haynes — a notorious gunman with a blood price on his head.

"Who'd profit by this boy's death?" he asked suddenly. "Does he have any enemies?"

"Tommy McCarty?" her voice was incredulous. "Goodness no! He was just sixteen, and there wasn't a finer boy in Peace Valley. Everyone liked him."

Carefully, he explained all that had happened, conscious of her skepticism and of the fact that she rode warily, with one hand on her pistol. "But who'd want to kill Tommy?" she exclaimed. "And why go to all that trouble? He rides alone to the claim every morning."

Except for the glaring lights of Rafe Landon's Sluice Box Bar and Doc Greenley's High-Stake Palace, the main street of the town was in darkness. But even before they reined in at the hitching rail of the High-Stake, the body had been seen, and a crowd gathered.

They were a sullen, hard-bitten crew of miners, gamblers, freighters, and drifters that follow gold camps. They crowded around shouting questions. Then suddenly Wade Manning pushed through, followed by Buff McCarty.

One glance, and the big man's face went white. "Tommy!" his voice was agonized, and he sprang forward to lift the body from the saddle.

He stared down into the boy's white, blood-stained face. When he looked up his placid features were set in hard, desperate lines. "Who did this?" he demanded.

With the crowd staring, Clip quietly told his story, helped by a word here and there from the girl, Ruth Manning. When the story was ended, Clip found himself ringed by a circle of hard, hostile eyes.

"Then," Buff McCarty said ominously, "you didn't see this feller up on the hill, eh? And Ruth didn't either. How do I know you didn't kill Tommy?"

"Yeah," a big man with a broken nose said loudly. "This stranger's yarn sounds fishy to me. The gal finds you all a standin' over the McCarty kid with a gun, an' —"

"Shut up, Porter!" Manning interrupted. "Let's hear him out."

"Why should I shoot the boy?" Clip protested. "I never saw the kid before. I don't shoot strangers."

"You say you heard shots, then rode up to him." Buff rested his big hands on his hips, his eyes hard. "Did anybody but you an' Ruth come nigh him?"

"Not a soul!" Clip said positively.

"Then," Buff's voice was harshly triumphant, "how d' you account for *this?*" He lifted an empty leather poke, shaking it in Haynes's face. "That there poke held three thousand dollars when my boy left town!"

The broken-nosed Porter crowded closer to

Clip. "You dirty, murderin' coyote!" he shouted, his face red with anger. "Y' oughta be lynched, dry-gulchin a kid that way!"

"That's right!" another voice yelled. "Lynch him!"

"Hold it!" Clip Haynes's voice was hard. His greenish eyes seemed to glow as he backed away. Suddenly, they saw he was holding two guns, although no man had seen him draw. "Manning, you an' McCarty ought to know better than this! Look at those wounds! That boy was shot with a rifle, not a six-gun! He was shot from higher up the mountain. You'll find both those wounds range downward! You come out to Indian Creek to offer me the job of lawman around here. Well, I took it, an' solvin' this murder is goin' t' be my first job. But just to clear the air, I'm a-tellin' all of you now, my name ain't Perry — it's *Clip Haynes!*"

He backed to his horse, stepped quickly around and threw himself into the saddle. Then he faced the crowd, now staring at him, white-faced. Beyond them, he saw Doc Greenley. The banker-saloon man was smiling oddly.

"I'll be around," Haynes said then, "an' I aim to complete the job I started. You all know who I am. But if anybody here thinks I'm the killer of that boy, he can talk it out with me tomorrow noon in this street — with six-guns!"

Clip Haynes wheeled the big black and rode rapidly away, and the crowd stood silent until he was out of sight. Then quietly they walked inside.

"What d' you think, Wade?" McCarty asked, turning to the tall, silent man beside him.

Manning was staring up the road after Haynes, a curious light in his eyes. "I think we'd better let him handle it," Wade said, "at least for the time. There's more in this than meets the eye!"

Doc Greenley walked up, rubbing his hands with satisfaction. "Just the man!" he said eagerly. "Did you see how he handled that? Just the man we need! We can make our shipment now when we want to, and that man will take care of it!"

Chapter 2
Man-Bait for the
Bushwhack Brothers

Dawn found Clip Haynes sitting among the boulders beside the trail from Indian Creek. Below him was the spot where Tommy McCarty had fallen the previous night. Opposite him, somewhere on the hillside, was the place where the murderer had waited. The very place of concealment was obvious enough. It was not a hundred yards away, in a cluster of boulders and rock cedar, not unlike his own resting place. That the murderer had waited there was undoubted, but why?

Clip Haynes pushed his hat back on his head and rolled a smoke.

First, what were the facts? McCarty, Greenley, and Manning, three of Basin City's most reputable business men, had hired him as marshal. But Rafe Landon, owner of the biggest mine, and the most popular saloon and dance hall, had not come along. Why?

Secondly, someone had killed and robbed Tommy McCarty. Obviously, the killer had not robbed him, for both Clip and Ruth Manning had been too close. Then, the obvious conclusion was that Tommy had been robbed before he was killed!

Clip sat up suddenly, his eyes narrowed. He

was remembering the chafed spot on Tommy's wrist, dimly seen in the light from the High-Stake Palace. Chafed from what? The answer hit him like a blow. Tommy McCarty had not only been robbed, but had been bound hand and foot! He had escaped, and then had been shot.

But why shoot him afterward? That didn't make sense. He already had lost the money, and if the thief had any doubts, he would have killed him the first time. The only answer was that Tommy McCarty had been mistaken for somebody else!

But who? Obviously, whoever had waited on the hillside the previous night had been expecting someone to come along. So far, Clip knew of only three people besides McCarty who might have come along. Wade Manning, Ruth Manning, and himself. But wait! What was Wade doing on the road so late? And why was Ruth traveling alone on that lonely trail?

There was always the possibility that Wade Manning, knowing Perry actually was Clip Haynes, had planned to kill him for the reward offered in Arizona. However, Manning didn't look like a cowardly killer, and the theory didn't, somehow, fit the facts.

Clip Haynes shook his head with disgust. If it was just a matter of shooting it out with some tough gunman, he was all right, but figuring out a problem like this was something he had not bargained for. It was unlikely, however, that anyone would want to shoot Ruth, or that anyone guessed she was on the road that night. That left Wade and himself as the prospective victims of the killer, for by now he would know his mistake.

Three men had known that he was taking the canyon trail to town — Doc Greenley, Wade Manning, and Buff McCarty. Clip's eyes narrowed. Why, since he had been riding slowly, and Tommy McCarty probably at a breakneck speed, hadn't Tommy passed him? Obviously because Tommy had come out on the trail at some point between where Clip had first heard his running horse and the point where he had seen the boy killed.

Mounting, Clip turned the big black down the mountainside to the trail. As he rode along he scanned the edges carefully. Suddenly, he reined in.

The hoof-prints of the big black were plainly seen, but suddenly a new trail had appeared, and Clip could see where a horse had been jumped from the embankment into the trail. Dismounting, and leading the black, he climbed the embankment and followed the trail. As soon as he saw it was plainly discernible, he swung into the saddle again and followed it rapidly.

Two miles from the canyon trail, at the end of a bottleneck canyon, he found a half-ruined adobe house. Here the trail ended.

Dismounting cautiously, Clip walked up to the 'dobe. The place was empty. Gun in hand, he knelt, examining the hardpacked earth of the floor.

The earth was scuffed and kicked as though by a pair of heels, such marks as a man might make in a struggle to free himself. But there were no ropes in sight, nothing. . . .

He froze. A shadow had fallen across him. He knew a man was crouching at the window behind him. His own gun was concealed from the watcher by his body. Apparently studying the earth, he waited for the first movement of the man behind him.

It could only have been an instant later that he heard the click of a cocking gun hammer, and in that same flashing split second, he hurled himself to one side. The roar of the gun boomed in the 'dobe hut, and the dirt against the wall jumped in an awkward spray even as his own pistol roared. Clip leaped to the door.

A bullet slammed against the doorjamb not an inch from his head, as he recklessly sprang into the open, both guns bucking. The man staggered, tried to fire again, and then plunged over on his face.

For a moment, Clip Haynes stood still, the light breeze brushing a lock of hair along his forehead. The sun felt warm against his cheek, and the silent figure on the sand looked sprawled and helpless.

Automatically, Clip loaded his guns. Then he walked over to the body. Before he knelt his eyes scanned the rim of the canyon, examining every boulder, every tree. Satisfied, he bent over the fallen man. Then his eyes narrowed thoughtfully.

It was the big man who had been so eager to see him lynched the night before, the man who had joined Porter in his protests.

Clip's eyes narrowed thoughtfully, then he got to his feet. He turned slowly, facing the shack. He stood there a moment carelessly, his thumbs hooked in his belt.

"All right," he said finally, "you can come out from behind that shack. With your hands high!"

Wade Manning stepped out, his hands up. His eyes glinted shrewdly. "Nice going," he said. "How did you know I was there?"

Clip shrugged, and indicated the big black horse with a motion of his head. "His ears. He doesn't miss a thing." He waited, his eyes cold.

"I suppose you want to know what I'm doing here?"

"Exactly. And what you were doing on the canyon trail last night. You seem to be around whenever there's any shooting going on."

"I can explain that," Wade said, smiling a little. "I don't blame you for being suspicious. After we talked to you at the mine that day, I decided I'd better go back out there and tell you I knew who you were, and to be careful around the men at the mine. And I didn't want you to jump to conclusions about Landon."

"What's Rafe Landon to you?" Clip demanded.

Wade shrugged, rolling a smoke. "Maybe I know men, maybe I don't," he affirmed, running his tongue along the paper. "But Rafe sizes up

104

to me like a square shooter." He glanced up. "And in spite of what Ruth says, I think you are too."

"Know this hombre?" Clip indicated the man on the ground.

Wade nodded. "Only to see him. He worked for Buff McCarty for a while. Lately he's been hanging around the Sluice Box. Name's Dirk Barlow. He's got a couple of tough-hand brothers."

Mounting, they started down the trail together. Clip Haynes glanced out of the corner of his eyes at Manning. He was clean cut, smooth, good-looking. His actions were suspicious, but he didn't seem the type for a killer.

Clip frowned a little. So Ruth didn't like him? Something stirred inside him, and he found himself wishing she felt differently. Then he grinned wryly. A hunted gunman like Clip Haynes getting soft about a girl! There wouldn't ever be any girls like Ruth for him.

He looked up, his mind reverting to the former problem. "How about this gent Porter back in town — the one who was so sure I shot Tommy McCarty. Where does he fit in?"

"A bad hombre. Gun-slick, and tough. He killed a prospector his first night in town. About two weeks later he shot it out with a man named Pete Handown."

"I've heard of Handown. This Porter must be fast."

"He is. But mostly a fistfighter. He runs with

the surviving Barlow brothers — Joe and Gonny. They're gunmen, too. They've figured in most of the trouble around here. But they've got a ringleader. Somebody behind the scenes we can't decide on."

"Greenley thinks it's Rafe, eh?"

"Yes. I'll admit most of the gang hang around the Sluice Box. But I'm sure Rafe's in the clear." Wade looked up. "Listen, Clip. If you ride with the stage tomorrow, watch your step. There's three hundred thousand in gold going out."

Doc Greenley was standing with Buff McCarty on the walk in front of the High-Stake Palace when they rode up. He glanced swiftly at the body slung over the lead horse. Then he smiled brightly. "Got 'em on the run, boy?" he asked. "Who is it this time?"

"Dirk Barlow," Buff said, his eyes narrowing. "You'll have to ride careful now, Haynes. His brothers will come for you. They're tough as hell."

Haynes shrugged. "He asked for it." His eyes lifted to Buff's. "I back-trailed Tommy. I knew he cut in ahead of me last night, and if you looked, there was a chafed spot on his wrist. I knew he'd been tied, so I looked for the place. I found it, and this hombre tried to kill me."

"You think he killed Tommy?" Buff demanded.

"I don't know. He hasn't the money on him." He turned his head to see Ruth Manning standing in front of the post office. Their eyes met, and she turned away abruptly.

Clip swung down from the saddle and walked across the street. When he stepped into the Sluice Box he saw Rafe Landon leaning against the end of the bar.

He was a tall man, handsome, and superbly built. There was an easy grace in his movements that was deceptive. He was wearing black, and when he turned, Clip saw he carried two guns, tied low.

"How are you, Haynes?" he said, holding out his hand. "I've been expecting you."

Haynes nodded. "What do you know about this McCarty killing?" he asked coolly. He deliberately ignored the outstretched hand.

Landon smiled. "An accident, of course. Nobody cared about hurting Tommy. He was a grand youngster."

"What d'you mean — an accident?"

"Just that. They were gunning for somebody else, but Tommy got there first." Rafe looked down at his cigarette, flicked off the ash, and glanced up. "In fact, it would be my guess they were gunning for you. Somebody who didn't want Clip Haynes butting in."

"Nobody knew I was Haynes."

Rafe shrugged. "I did. I'd known for two weeks. Manning knew too. Probably there were others." He nodded toward the street. "I see you got Dirk Barlow. Watch those brothers of his. And look out for Porter, too."

"You're the second man who told me that."

"There'll be more. Joe and Gonny Barlow will be in as soon as they hear about this. Joe's bad, but Gonny's the worst. Gonny uses both hands, and he's fast."

"Why tell me this?" Clip asked. He looked up, and their eyes met.

Rafe Landon smiled. "You'll need it, Haynes. I'm a gambler, and it's my business to know about men. A word of friendly advice never hurt anyone — even a gent like you. Joe Barlow's never been beat in a gunfight. And like I said, Gonny's the worst."

"Porter? What's he like?" Clip asked.

"Maybe I can tell you," a harsh voice broke in.

Clip turned to see Porter standing in the doorway. He was big, probably twenty pounds bigger than Clip, and his shoulders were powerful.

"All right," Clip said. "You tell me."

Chapter 3
The Barlows
Strike

Porter walked over to the bar.

Glancing past him Clip could see the room filling with men. Come to see the fun, to see if the new marshal could take it. Clip grinned suddenly.

"What's funny?" Porter snarled suspiciously.

"You," Clip said shortly. "Last night I thought I heard you say I needed lynching. I suggested anyone who wanted to debate the matter could shoot it out with me in the street. You weren't around. What's the matter? Yellow?"

Porter stared, taken aback by the sudden attack. Somebody chuckled, and he let out a snarl of rage. "Why you — !"

Clip's open palm slapped him across the mouth with such force that Porter's head jerked back.

With a savage roar, the big man swung. But Clip was too fast. Swaying on his feet, he slipped the punch and smashed a vicious right hand into the man's body. Porter took it without flinching, and swung both hands to Clip's head.

Haynes staggered, and before he could set himself Porter swung a powerful right that knocked him sprawling. Before Clip could get to his feet,

Porter rushed in, kicking viciously at Haynes's face, but the young marshal jerked his head aside and took the kick on the shoulder. The camel boot sent pain shocks through his body.

It knocked him rolling, but he gathered his feet under him and met Porter's charge with a jarring left jab that set the bigger man back on his heels and smashed his upper lip into his teeth.

Porter ducked his head and charged, but Clip was steadying down, and he sidestepped suddenly, bringing up a jolting right uppercut that straightened Porter up for a crashing right that knocked him reeling into the bar.

He grabbed a bottle and hurled it across the room, but Clip ducked and charged in, grabbing the big man about the knees and dropping him to the floor. Deliberately, Clip fell with him, driving his head into the man's stomach with all his force, and then spinning on over to land on his feet.

Breathing easily, he waited until Porter got up. The big man was dazed, and before he could assemble his faculties, Clip walked in and slapped him viciously with both hands, and then snapped his fist into Porter's solar plexus with a jolt that doubled the bigger man up with a groan. A left hook spun him half around and ripped the skin under one eye. As he backed away, trying to cover, Clip walked in and pulled his hands away, crossing a wicked short right hook to the chin. Without a sound, Porter crumpled to the floor.

Turning on his heel, Clip walked quickly from

the room, never so much as glancing back.

It was almost noon when he rode slowly down the mountain trail and tied his horse in a clump of mesquite. He glanced at the sun. In about fifteen minutes the stage should be along, and if it was to be held up, it would be somewhere in the next two miles. Carefully, he walked ahead until he found a place among the boulders, and then settled down to wait until the stage came along. From there on he could follow it.

Suddenly, he noticed a cloud of dust above the trail in the distance. The stage. He got up, and stood watching it as it drew nearer. He could see that everything was as it should be, and turning, he walked back to his horse. When he was about a dozen steps away, he halted in midstep, and drew back. There on the ground, over one of his own tracks was a fresh boot-print, one heel rounded badly, and a queer scar across the toe!

His hand shot to his gun, but before he could draw, something crashed down over his head, and he tumbled forward into blackness. . . .

It was hours later when he opened his eyes. When he tried to lift his head a spasm of pain shot over him, and he groaned desperately. Then for a long moment he lay still, and through the wave of pain from his throbbing head, he remembered the stage, the boot print, the gold.

Desperately, he got to his hands and knees. The ground where his head had lain was a pool of blood, and when he lifted one hand, he found his hair matted with it and stiffened with sand.

Crawling to his feet, he had to steady himself against a boulder. Then he retched violently, and was sick.

After he staggered to his horse and took a drink from his canteen, he felt better. Summoning all his resolution, he went back and examined the ground. The man had evidently followed him, waited behind a boulder, and as he returned to his horse, knocked him over the head. Quite obviously, he had been left for dead.

Clip walked back to his horse, checking his guns. They hadn't been tampered with. When he swung into the saddle and turned the big black down the trail, his lips were set in a tight, grim line. He loosened the big guns, and despite his throbbing head, cantered down the trail.

He didn't have far to ride. Only about three hundred yards from where he had waited, he found the coach, lying on its side, one wheel smashed. A dead horse lay in a tangle of harness, and sprawled on the ground was the stage driver. He had been shot between the eyes with a rifle.

About twenty yards away, evidently killed as he was making for the shelter of a circle of boulders, was the messenger.

It was two hours before Clip Haynes rode up in front of the High-Stake Palace and tied the black to the hitching rail. His head throbbing, he stepped in.

At once the hard round muzzle of a gun jammed into his spine.

Clip stopped, his hands slowly lifting.

"Back up, an' back careful!" he heard Buff McCarty saying, his voice deadly. "One false move an' I'll drill you, gunman or no gunman!"

"What's the matter, Buff?" Clip asked. His head throbbed and he felt his anger mounting.

"You ask what's the matter!" Wade Manning snapped. Stepping up he jerked Clip's guns from their holsters. "We trusted you, and then you —"

"We found the money, that's what!" Buff snarled, his voice husky with rage. "The money you took off Tommy! We shook down your duffle bag an' found it there — the whole three thousand dollars you murdered him for!"

"Listen, men!" he protested. "If you found any money there it was a plant. Why —"

"I'm sorry, boy," Doc Greenley interrupted, shaking his head gravely, his usual smile gone. "We've got you dead to rights this time!"

Clip started to protest again, and then his jaw clamped shut. If they wanted to be like that, argument, he figured, was useless. He turned to walk out, and found himself facing Porter.

The big man sneered, and, for just an instant as Clip watched him, he saw the man's eyes flash a message to one of his captors. Then Porter was past, and Clip was being rushed to jail.

When the cell door clanged shut he walked across the narrow room, dropped on his bunk and was almost immediately asleep.

It seemed a long time later when he was awakened. It was completely dark, and listening, he knew the jail was deserted.

Clip walked across to the window, and took hold of the bars.

Then h heard a whisper. "Haynes!"

"Who is it?" he asked softly.

"It's me — Rafe. Stick your hand through the bars. I've got a key!"

Clip Haynes thrust his hand out, and felt the cold metal of a jail key in his hand. Then he heard Rafe speaking again. "Better make it quick. Porter's got a mob about worked up lynching you."

In two strides he was across the cell. The key grated in the lock, and the door swung wide. Then he turned and stepped back, throwing the blankets into a rough hump to resemble a sleeping figure. Going out, he locked the door after him. His gun belts were on the desk in the outer office, and he swept them up, hurriedly checking the guns he stepped outside.

Rafe Landon was waiting there. Surprisingly, Rafe had the black horse with him. Without a word, Clip gripped the gambler's hand, and then swung up.

"Listen," Rafe said, gripping his wrist. "Whoever robbed that stage today kidnaped Ruth!"

"What!" Clip jerked around, his jaws set.

"She rode out along the trail just before the stage left town. She told me she wanted to watch you. She hasn't returned yet, and Wade's just found out. There's only one place she can be — with the Barlows!"

"You know where they hang out?" Clip snapped.

"Somewhere back of the Organ. There's a box canyon up there, that might be it. Take the west route around the Organ and you'll find the trail, but watch your step!"

Clip looked down at Rafe in the darkness, his eyes keen. "Just what is Ruth Manning to you?" he demanded.

Clip thought he detected the ghost of a smile. "Does it matter? The girl's in danger!"

"Right!" Clip swung his horse. As he did so he heard someone shout, and glancing back, he saw a crowd of men spew from the doors of the High-Stake.

The big black stretched his legs and sprang away into the night, swinging around the town to the trail in tireless, space-eating strides.

Chapter 4
Gun Law Comes
to Basin City

The huge pinnacles of rock known as the Organ loomed ahead. For years during his wanderings, Clip Haynes had heard of them. Some queer volcanic effect had shot these hollow spires up into the sky, leaving them thin to varying degrees, and under the blows of a stick or rock they gave forth a deep, resonant sound. Around them lay rugged, broken country.

For a half hour he cut back and forth through the rocks before he located the box canyon. And then it was the horse that found the narrow thread of trail winding among the boulders. A few minutes of riding, and he sighted the dim light which came from a cabin window.

He dismounted and slipped a gun into his hand. Then he walked boldly forward, and threw the door open.

A startled Mexican jerked up from his seat on a box and dropped a hand for his gun, but at the sight of Clip, he reached for air. "Don't shoot, señor!" he gasped. "*Por dios*, don't shoot!"

Clip stepped in and swung his back to the wall. "Where's the girl?" he snapped.

"The señorita, she here. The Barlows, they go."

Clip stepped quickly across the room and spun the Mexican around. Picking up a handful of loose rope, he bound the man hand and foot. Then stooping, he untied Ruth.

"Thanks," she said, rubbing her wrists. "I was beginning to think —"

"No!" he exclaimed dryly.

Her face stiffened abruptly. Clip grinned at her. "You had that coming, lady. Let's get out of here!"

Suddenly, he stopped. In the corner was a heap of sacks taken from the stage earlier that day. Pausing, he jerked the tie string. The sack toppled slowly over. And from its mouth spilled nothing more than a thin stream of sand!

"Why — !" Ruth gasped. "Why, where's the gold?"

"I'll show you later!" Clip said grimly. "I suspected this!"

There was no talk on the ride homeward. Clip rode at Ruth's side, seemingly intent only on reaching town. It was almost daylight when they rode swiftly up the dusty street.

"Should you do this?" she protested. "Aren't they looking for you?"

"If they are, they better not find me!" he snapped. "I'm doing some looking myself. You ride to your brother, quick, and tell him about that sand. Tell him to bring Buff McCarty to the High-Stake just as quick as he can make it!"

His eyes narrowed. "And you," he went on grimly, "will have a chance to drop by the Sluice

Box and see your precious lover, who didn't have guts enough to come after you himself!"

Her eyes widened with amazement, but before she could speak, he wheeled his horse and rode rapidly back up the street and dismounted. Then he walked into the Sluice Box, his face dark with rage.

Rafe Landon stood just inside the door. He walked up to Clip, smiling gravely. "I heard what you said to Ruth," he said. "I want to tell you just two things, Haynes. The first has to do with my want of — guts — as you put it. Once I offered you my hand, and you refused it. Will you take it now?"

Something in his manner seemed strange. Clip glanced down at the gloved hand. Then he took it. Amazement came into his eyes.

"Yes," Rafe said, "you're right. It's iron. The blacksmith in Goldfield made it, several years ago. I lost both my hands after a fire."

Clip looked up, his face tight. "Rafe, I —"

"Forget it. As for Ruth —"

The doors burst open, and Clip wheeled. Wade Manning stood in the door, Buff McCarty beside him. "The Barlows are coming!" he exclaimed, his face tense. "Both of them, Clip, and they've been bragging all morning that they'll kill you on sight!"

He stepped into the street, his steps echoing hollowly as he stepped across the boardwalk. He stopped in the edge of the dusty street and looked north.

The Barlows, Joe and Gonny, were standing on the porch in front of the old hotel building. Then they saw him, and started toward the steps.

Somewhere a horse whinnied, and in the saloon, a man's nervous laughter sounded strangely loud. Clip Haynes walked slowly, taking measured steps.

Joe Barlow's hand was poised over his gun. Gonny waited carelessly, slouching, a shock of hair hanging down over his eyes.

When they were fifty feet apart, the Barlows stiffened as though at a signal, and drew. Joe's hand moved; Clip Haynes shot.

The street broke in a thundering roar through which he found himself walking straight toward them, his guns hammering. He knew the first shot he had taken at Joe had been too quick. Suddenly it seemed as if a white hot branding iron had hit his left shoulder. He dropped that gun, feeling the warm blood run down his sleeve. His arm was useless — but his right gun kept firing.

Suddenly, Joe was falling from the steps, and almost as in a dream Clip saw the man straighten out, arms widespread, blood staining the dust beneath him.

Clip started to step forward, and realized suddenly that he was on his knees. He got up, feeling another slug hit him in the side. Gonny was facing him, legs spread wide, a fire-blossoming gun in either hand. A streak of red crossed his jaw.

Clip started toward him, holding his last bullet. Something slanted a rapier of pain along his ribs, and one of his legs tried to buckle, but still Clip held his fire. Then, suddenly, about a dozen feet away from Gonny, Clip Haynes turned loose his gun.

Almost before his eyes Gonny's gray flannel shirt turned into a crimson, sodden mass. The gunman started to fall, caught himself, and lifted a gun. They were almost body to body when the shot flamed in Clip's face. Something struck him a terrific blow on the side of the head, and he fell. . . .

Actually it was only a minute, but it seemed hours. Men were running from every direction, and as Clip Haynes caught at somebody's leg and pulled his bloody body erect, he heard Wade gabbling in his ear. But he didn't stop. It was only a dozen feet, but it seemed a mile. Step by step, he made it, fumbling shells into his gun.

Weaving on his feet, he stopped, facing Doc Greenley. His eyes wavered, then they focused.

Doc's face went sickly with fear. He opened and closed his mouth, trying to speak. Then suddenly he broke, and went for his gun.

It was just swinging level when Clip shot him. Then Clip pitched over on his face, and lay still.

He must have been a long time coming out of it because they were all there — Ruth, Rafe Landon, Wade Manning, and Buff McCarty — when he opened his eyes. He looked from one to the other.

"Doc?" he questioned weakly.

"You got him, Clip. We found the gold in his safe. He never moved an ounce of it, just sand. We made Porter confess. He robbed Tommy of the three thousand dollars, and later Doc Greenley made him plant it on you. One of the Barlows slugged you.

"We found the note you left in the jail. You were right. It was Doc who killed Tommy, trying to kill you. He didn't know you were Clip Haynes at first.

"I told him," Wade continued, "never suspecting he was the guilty one behind all this. He knew he couldn't fool you. Felt he'd given himself away somehow. He confessed before he died."

Clip nodded. "At first — at the mine. He said Clip Haynes got ten thousand. Only the law and the bandits knew it was that much." Clip paused, a wan smile twisting his features. "He was the one planned that job — not Haynes. I was the law. The express company hired me. When he said that, I was suspicious."

Clip closed his eyes, and lay very still. When he opened them again everyone was gone but Ruth. She was smiling, and she leaned over and kissed him gently on the lips.

"And Rafe?" he questioned.

"I tried to explain, but you ran away. He's my uncle — my mother's brother. He started Wade in business here, but no one knew. He thought it might hurt Wade if people knew a gambler backed him."

"Oh," he said. For a moment he was silent. Then he looked up, and they both smiled.

"That's nice," he said.

SHANDY
TAKES THE HOOK

For three days Shandy Gamble had been lying on his back in the Perigord House awaiting the stranger in the black mustache. Nichols, his name was, and if they were ever going to start cattle buying they had better be moving. The season was already late.

Shandy Gamble was seventeen years old and tall for his age. In fact, he was tall for any age. Four inches over six feet, he was all feet, hands, and shoulders. With his shirt off you could count every rib in his lean body.

Perigord was the biggest town Shandy had ever seen. In fact, it was only the third town he had seen in his life. With the cattle buyers in town there was most a thousand head of folks, and on the street Shandy felt uncomfortable and mighty crowded. Most of his time he spent down at the horse corrals or lying on his bed waiting for Nichols.

He had come to town to buy himself a new saddle and bridle. Maybe a new hat and shirt. He was a saving man, Shandy Gamble was, despite his youth. Now he not only was holding his own money but five hundred dollars belonging to Nichols. Had it not been for that he wouldn't have waited, for by now he was homesick for the KT outfit.

Nichols was a big, powerful man with a smooth

shaved face and black, prominent eyes. He also had black hair and a black mustache. Shandy had been leaning on the corral gate when Nichols approached him.

"Good afternoon, sir!" Nichols thrust out a huge hand. "I understand you're a cattleman?"

Shandy Gamble blinked. Nobody had ever called him a cattleman before and his chest swelled appreciably. He was a forty-dollar-a-month cowhand, although at the moment he did have five hundred and fifty-two dollars in his pocket.

Fifty-two dollars was saved from his wages, and the five hundred was half the reward money for nailing two horse thieves back in the cedar country. Shandy had tracked them back there for Deputy Sheriff Holloway, and then when they killed Holloway he got mad and went in after them. He brought one out dead and one so badly mauled he wished he was dead. There was a thousand dollars on their heads and Shandy tried to give it to Mrs. Holloway, but she would accept only half.

Shandy shifted uneasily on the bed. It was time Nichols got back. The proposition had sounded good, no question about that. "You can't beat it, Gamble," Nichols had said. "You know cattle and I've the connections in Kansas City and Chicago. We can ride over the country buying cattle, then ship and sell them. A nice profit for both of us."

"That would take money, and I ain't got

much," Shandy had said.

Nichols eyed him thoughtfully. No use telling the boy he had seen that roll when Shandy paid for his room in advance. "It won't take much to start," Nichols scowled as he considered the size of Shandy's roll. "Say a thousand dollars."

"Shucks," Shandy was regretful. "I ain't got but five hundred."

"Fine!" Nichols clapped him on the shoulder. "We're partners then! You put up five hundred and I'll put up five hundred! We'll bank that here, and then start buying. I've got unlimited credit east of here, and when the thousand is gone, we'll draw on that. At this stage you'll be the one doing most of the thinking, so you won't need to put as much cash into it as I do."

"Well —" Shandy was not sure. It sounded like a good deal, and who knew cows better than he did? He had been practically raised with cows. "Maybe it would be a good deal. Old Ed France has a herd nobody's looked at, nice, fat stock, too."

"Good!" Nichols clapped him on the shoulder again. From his pocket he took a long brown envelope and a sheaf of bills. Very carefully he counted off five hundred dollars and stuck it into the envelope. "Now your five hundred."

Shandy dug down and hauled out his bills and counted off the five hundred dollars and tucked it into the envelope.

"Now," Nichols started to put the envelope in his pocket, "we'll go to the bank, and —"

He stopped, then withdrew the envelope. "No, you just keep this on you. We'll bank it later."

Shandy Gamble accepted the fat envelope and stuck it into his shirt. Nichols glanced at his watch then rubbed his jaw. "Tell you what," Nichols said, "I've got to catch the stage for Holbrook. I'll be back tomorrow night. You stick around and don't let this money out of your hands, whatever you do. I'll see you at the hotel."

Shandy watched him go, shrugged, and went back to watching the horses. There was a fine black gelding there. Now if he was a cattle buyer, he would own that gelding, buy the new saddle and bridle, and some fancy clothes like Jim Finnegan wore, and would he show that outfit back on the KT!

The wait had dampened his enthusiasm. Truth was, he liked the KT and liked working with the boys. They were a good outfit. He rolled over on the bed and swung his feet to the floor. Reaching for his boots he shoved his big feet into them and stood up.

To blazes with it! He'd open the envelope, leave the money in the bank for Nichols, and go back to the outfit. He was no cattle buyer, anyway. He was a cowhand.

Taking out the brown envelope, he ripped it open. Slowly he turned cold and empty inside, and stood there, his jaw slack, his shock of corn silk hair hanging over his face. The envelope was stuffed with old newspapers.

The spring grass faded from green to brown and dust gathered in the trails. Water holes shrank and the dried earth cracked around them and the cattle grew gaunt. It was a hard year on the caprock, and that meant work for the hands.

Shandy Gamble was in the saddle eighteen to twenty hours most days, rounding up strays and pushing them south to the gullies and remaining water holes. When he had returned without his saddle there was a lot of jawing about it, and the boys all poked fun at Shandy, but he grinned widely and took it, letting them believe he had drunk it up or spent it on women.

Jim Finnegan rode out one day on a gray horse. He was looking the situation over and making estimates on the beef to be had after the fall roundup. Shandy was drifting south with three head of gaunted stock when they met. Gamble drew up and Finnegan joined him. "Howdy, son! Stock looks poor."

"Yeah," Shandy dug for the makings, "we need rain plumb bad." He rolled his smoke, then asked quietly, "You ever hear of a buyer name of Nichols? Big, black-eyed man?"

Shandy's description was accurate and painstaking, the sort of description a man might give who was used to reading sign and who thirty seconds after a glimpse of a horse or cow could describe its every hair and ailment.

"Nichols? You've forgotten the name, son. No, the hombre you describe is Abel Kotch. He's a card slick an' confidence man. Brute of a fighter, too. Brags he never saw the man could stand up to him in a fist fight."

"Seen him around?"

"Yeah, he was around Fort Worth earlier this year. He rousts around with the June boys."

The June boys. There were five of the Junes — the old man, Pete June, and the four outlaw sons: Alec, Tom, Buck, and Windy. All were gun slicks, bad men, dirty, unkempt drifters, known to be killers, believed to be horse and cow thieves, and suspected of some out and out murders.

Two nights later, back at the bunkhouse, Johnny Smith rode in with the mail, riding down from Tuckup way where he had stopped to ask after some iron work being done for the ranch by the Tuckup blacksmith. Tuckup was mostly an outlaw town, but the blacksmith there was the best around. Cowhands do most of their own work, but the man at Tuckup could make anything with iron, and the KT boss had been getting some fancy andirons for his fireplace.

"Killin' over to Tuckup," Johnny said, as he swung down. "That Sullivan from Brady Canyon tangled with Windy June. Windy bored him plenty."

Shandy Gamble's head came up. "June? The rest of that outfit there?"

"Sure, the whole shootin' match o' Junes!"

"Big, black-eyed fellow with 'em? Black mustache?"

"Kotch? Sure as you know he is. He whupped

130

the blacksmith. Beat him so bad he couldn't finish the old man's andirons. That's a rough outfit."

The hoss of the KT was talking to Jim Finnegan when Shandy strolled up. "Boss, anything you want done over Tuckup way? I got to ride over there."

The Boss glanced at him sharply. It was unlike Gamble to ask permission to be away from his work. He was a good hand, and worked like two men. If he wanted to go to Tuckup there was a reason.

"Yeah. Ask about my irons. Too, you might have a look up around the water pocket. We're missin' some cows. If you find them, or see any suspicious tracks, come ahootin' an' we'll ride up that way."

Shandy Gamble was astride a buckskin that belonged to the KT. He was a short coupled horse with a wide head, good at cutting or roping, but a good trail horse, too. Johnny Smith, who was mending a bridle, glanced up in time to see Gamble going out of the door with his rifle in his hand. That was not too unusual, with plenty of wolves and lions around, but Shandy was wearing two guns, something that hadn't happened for a long time. Johnny's brow puckered, then he shrugged and went back to work on the bridle.

The Tuckup Trail was a scar across the face of the desert. It was a gash in the plateau, and everywhere was rock, red rock, pink rock, white, yellow, and buff rock, twisted and gnarled into weird shapes. By night it was a ghost land where a wide moon floated over the blasted remains of ancient mountains, and by day it was an oven blazing with heat and dancing with dust devils and heat-waved distance.

Tuckup was a cluster of shabby down-at-heel buildings tucked back into a hollow among the rocks. It boasted that there was a grave in boot hill for every living person in town, and they always had two empty graves waiting to receive the next customers.

Tuckup was high, and despite the blazing heat of the day, a fire was usually welcome at night. The King High Saloon was the town's resort, meeting place, and hang-out. Second only to it was the stable, a rambling, gloomy building full of stalls for sixty horses and a loft full of hay.

Shandy Gamble stabled his horse and gave it a good rubdown. It had a hard ride ahead of it, for he knew that there would be no remaining in town after he had done what he had to do.

Lean, gangling, and slightly stooped, he stood in the stable door and rolled a smoke. His shoulders seemed excessively broad above the narrow hips, and the two .44's hung with their butts wide and easy to his big hands. He wore jeans and a faded checkered shirt. His hat was gray, dusty and battered. There was a hole through the crown that one of the horse thieves had put there.

There was the saloon, a general store, the blacksmith shop, and livery stable. Beyond and around was a scattering of a dozen or so houses, mostly mere shacks. Then there were two bunkhouses that called themselves hotels.

Shandy Gamble walked slowly across to the blacksmith shop. The smith was a burly man, and when he looked up, Shandy saw a deep half-healed cut on his cheekbone and an eye still swollen and dark. "KT irons ready?" Shandy asked, to identity himself.

"Will be." The smith stared at him. "Rider from there just here yestiddy. Your boss must be in a mighty hurry."

"Ain't that. I had some business over here. Know an hombre name of Kotch?"

The smith glared. "You bein' funny?"

"No. I got business with him."

"Trouble?"

"Uh-huh. I'm goin' to beat his head in."

The smith shrugged. "Try it if you want. I done tried but not no more. He durned near kilt me."

"He won't kill me."

"Your funeral. He's up at the King High." The smith looked at him. "You be keerful. Them Junes is up there, too." He wiped his mustache. "KT, you better think again. You're only a kid."

"My feet make as big tracks as his'n."

"Goin' in, they may. Comin' out they may be a sight smaller."

Shandy Gamble's eyes were chill. "Like you

133

said, it's my funeral."

He hitched his guns in place and started across the street. He was almost to the hitch rail in front of the King High when he saw a fresh hide hung over the fence. It was still bloody. Curiously, he walked back. The brand had been cut away from the rest of the hide. Poking around in a pile of refuse ready for burning, he found it, scraped it clean, and tucked it into his pocket. He was turning when he looked up to see a man standing near him.

He was several inches shorter than Shandy, but he was wide and blocky. He wore his gun tied down and he looked mean. His cheeks were hollow and his eyes small. "What you doin', pokin' around here?"

"Just lookin'." Shandy straightened to his full height. "Sort of proddin' around."

"Whar you from?"

"Ridin' for the KT."

The man's lips tightened. "Git out of here!"

"Don't aim to be in no hurry."

"You know who I am? I'm Tom June, an' when I say travel, I mean it!"

Shandy stood looking at him, his eyes mild. "Well, now. Tom June, I've heard o' you. Heard you was a cow thief an' a rustler."

"Why, you — !" His hand swept for his gun, but Shandy had no idea to start a shooting now. His long left slammed out, his fist balled and rock hard. It caught Tom June flush on the mouth as his hand swept back for his gun and his head came forward. At the same time, Shandy's right swung into the pit of the man's stomach and his left dropped to the gun wrist.

The struggle was brief, desperate, and final. Shandy clubbed a big fist to the man's temple and he folded. Hurriedly, Shandy dragged him into a shed, disarmed and tied him. The last job he did well. Then he straightened and walked back to the street.

A quick glance up and down, and then he went up the steps to the porch in front of the King High Saloon, and through the batwing doors.

Five men sat around a poker game. Shandy recognized the broad back instantly as that of Nichols, who he now knew was Abel Kotch. At least two of the others were Junes, as he could tell from their faces.

Shoving his hat back on his head he stood behind Kotch and glanced down at his cards. Kotch had a good hand. The stack of money before him would come to at least two hundred dollars.

"Bet 'em," Shandy said.

Kotch stirred irritably in his chair. "Shut up!" he said harshly.

Shandy's gun was in his hand, the muzzle against Kotch's ear. "Bet 'em, I said. Bet 'em strong."

Kotch's hands froze. The Junes looked up, staring at the gangling, towheaded youth. "Beat it, kid!" he said sharply.

"You stay out of this, June!" Shandy Gamble's

voice was even. "My argyment's with this coyote. I'd as soon blow his head off as not, but if'n he does what he's told the worst he'll get is a beatin'!"

Kotch shoved chips into the center of the table. The Junes looked at their cards and raised. Kotch bet them higher. He won. Carefully, he raked in the coin.

"This is Shandy Gamble, Kotch. You owe me five hundred. Count it out before I forget myself an' shoot you, anyway."

"There ain't five hundred here!" Kotch protested.

"There's better'n four. Count it!"

"Well, what do you know, Windy?" The thin man grinned across the table. "Ole Kotch run into the wrong hombre for once! Wished Buck was here to see this!"

Reluctantly, Kotch counted the money. It came to four hundred and ten dollars. Coolly, Shandy Gamble pocketed the money. "All right," he said, "stand up mighty careful an' unload your pockets."

"What?" Kotch's face was red with fury. "I'll kill you for this!"

"Empty 'em. I want more money. I want a hundred an' twenty dollars more."

"You ain't got it comin'!" Kotch glared at him.

"Five hundred an' interest for one year at six per cent. You get it for me or I'll be forced to take your horse an' saddle."

"Why, you — !"

The gun lifted slightly and Abel Kotch shut up. His eyes searched the boy's face and what he read there wasn't pleasant. Kotch decided suddenly that this youngster would shoot, and shoot fast.

Carefully, he opened a money belt and counted out the hundred and twenty dollars which Gamble quietly stowed in his pockets. Then he holstered his gun and hitched the belts into place. "Now, just for luck, Mr. Cattle Buyer, I'm goin' to give you a lickin'!"

Kotch stared. "Why, you fool! You — !" He saw the fist coming and charged, his weight slamming Shandy back against the wall, almost knocking the wind from him. Kotch jerked a knee up to Gamble's groin, but the boy had grown up in cow camps and cattle towns, cutting his fighting teeth on the bone-hard, rawhide-tough teamsters of the freight outfits. Gamble twisted and threw Kotch off balance, then hit him with a looping right that staggered the heavier man.

Kotch was no flash in the pan. He could fight and he knew it. He set himself, feinted, and then threw a hard right that caught the boy flush on the chin. Shandy staggered but recovered as Kotch rushed and dropping his head, butted the heavier man under the chin. Kotch staggered, swinging both hands; and straightening, Shandy walked into him slugging.

They stood there wide legged and slugged like madmen, their ponderous blows slamming and battering at head and body. Shandy's head sang with the power of those punches and his breath came in gasps, but he was lean and hard from years of work on the range, and he fell into a rhythm of punching. His huge fists smashed at the gambler like battering rams.

Kotch was triumphant, then determined, then doubtful. His punches seemed to be soaked up by the boy's abundant vitality, while every time one of those big fists landed it jarred him to the toes. Suddenly he gave ground and swung a boot toe for Shandy's groin.

Turning, Gamble caught it on his leg, high up, then grabbed the boot and jerked. Kotch other foot lost the ground and he hit the floor hard. Gamble grabbed him by the shirt front and smashed him in the face, a free swing that flattened the bone in Kotch's nose. Then, jerking him erect, Shandy gripped him with his left hand and swung a looping blow to the wind. Kotch's knees buckled, and Shandy smashed him in the face again and again. Then he shoved him hard. Kotch staggered, brought up against the back wall, and slid to a sitting position, his face bloody, his head loose on its neck.

Shandy Gamble drew back and hitched his belts into place again. He mopped his face with a handkerchief, while he got his breath back. There were five men in the room now, all enemies without doubt. Two of them were Junes — obviously from earlier conversation they were Windy and Alec.

Shandy hitched his gun belts again and left his

138

thumbs tucked in them. He looked at Windy June. "Found a cowhide out back," he said, casually, "carried a KT brand."

Instantly, the room was still. Windy June was staring at him, his eyes ugly. Alec was standing with his right hand on the edge of the bar; the others spread suddenly, getting out of the way. This, then, was between himself and the Junes.

"What then?" Windy asked, low voiced.

"Your brother Tom didn't like it. I called him a rustler, and he didn't like that."

"You called Tom June a rustler?" Windy's voice was low with amazement. "And you're alive?"

"I took his gun away an' tied him up. I'm takin' him to the sheriff."

"You're takin' — why, you fool kid!"

"I'm takin' him, an' as you Junes ride together, I reckon you an' Alec better come along, too."

Windy June was astonished. Never in his life had he been called like this, and here, in his own bailiwick, by a kid. But then he remembered the job this kid had done on Abel Kotch and his lips grew close and tight.

"You better git," he said, "while you're all in one piece!"

The bartender spoke. "Watch yourself, Windy. I know this kid. He's the one that brought the boys in from Cottonwood, one dead an' one almost."

Windy June smiled thinly. "Look, kid. We don't want to kill you. There's two of us. If you get by us, there's still Buck an' Pop. You ain't got a chance with me alone, let alone the rest of them."

Shandy Gamble stood tall in the middle of the floor. His long face was sober. "You better come along then, Windy, because I aim to take you in, dead or alive!"

Windy June's hand was a blur of speed. Guns thundered and the walls echoed their thunder. In the close confines of the saloon a man screamed. There was the acrid smell of gunpowder and Shandy Gamble weaving in the floor's middle, his guns stabbing flame. He fired, then moved forward. He saw Alec double over and sprawl across Windy's feet, his gun sliding across the floor.

Windy, like a weaving blade of steel, faced Shandy and fired. Gamble saw Windy June's body jerk with the slam of a .44, saw it jerk again and twist, saw him going to his knees with blood gushing from his mouth, his eyes bitterly, wickedly alive, and the guns in his big fists hammering their futile bullets into the floor. Then Shandy fired again, and Windy June sprawled across Alec and lay still. In the moment of silence that followed the cannonading of the guns, Windy's foot twitched and his spur jingled.

Shandy Gamble faced the room, his eyes searching the faces of the other men. "I don't want no trouble from you. Two of you load the bodies on their horses. I'm taking 'em with me, like I said."

Abel Kotch sat on the floor, his shocked and bloody face stunned with amazement at the bodies that lay there. He had taken milk from a kitten and had it turn to a raging mountain lion before his eyes. He sat very still. He was out of this. He wanted to stay out. He was going to make no move that could be misinterpreted.

Slowly, they took the bodies out and tied them on the horses of the two June boys. Shandy watched them, then walked across to the stable to get his own horse, his eyes alert for the other Junes.

When he had the horses he walked back to the shed and saw Tom June staring up at him.

"What, happened? I heard shootin'?"

"Yeah."

Shandy reached down and caught him by his jacket collar with his left hand and coolly dragged him out of the shed, his feet dragging. He took him to the front of the saloon and threw him bodily across his horse. The bound man saw the two bodies, dripping and bloody. He cried out, then began to swear, viciously and violently.

"Look out, kid."

Who spoke, he did not know, but Shandy Gamble glanced up and saw two other men who wore the brand of the June clan — Pop and Buck June — wide apart in the street. Their fires were set and ready.

Shandy Gamble stepped away from the horses into the street's center. "You can drop your guns an' come with me!" he called.

Neither man spoke. They came on, steadily and inexorably. And then something else happened. Up the street behind them appeared a cavalcade of riders, and Shandy recognized his boss, leading them. Beside him rode Johnny Smith and Jim Finnegan and behind them the riders from the KT.

"Drop 'em, June!" The boss's voice rang out sharp and clear. "There's nine of us here. No use to die!"

The Junes stopped. "No use, Buck," Pop June said, "the deck's stacked agin us."

The boss rode on past and stopped. He stared at the dead Junes and the bound body of Tom. He looked at Shandy as if he had never seen him before.

"What got into you, Shandy?" he asked. "We'd never have known, but Johnny told us when you heard the Junes were here you got your guns and left. Then Jim remembered you'd been askin' him about this here Kotch, who trailed with 'em."

Shandy shrugged, building a smoke. "Nothin'. We'd had trouble, Kotch an' me." He drew the patch of hide from his pocket. "Then there was this, out back. Tom started a ruction when he seen me find it."

Shandy Gamble swung into his saddle. "I reckon the Junes'll talk, an' they'll tell you where the cows are. An' boss," Shandy puckered his brow, "could I ride into Perigord? I want to git me a new saddle."

"You got the money?" The boss reached for his pocket.

"Yeah," Shandy smiled, "I got it from Kotch. He'd been holdin' it for me."

"Holdin' it for him!" Finnegan exploded. "He trusted Kotch — with money?"

Kotch had come to the door and was staring out at them. The boss chuckled. "Well, trust or not, looks like he collected!"

NO MAN'S MAN

I

He came to a dirty cantina on a fading afternoon. He stood, looking around with a curious eye. And he saw me there in the corner, my back to the wall and a gun on the table, and my left hand pouring tequila into a glass.

He crossed the room to my table, a man with a scholar's face and a quiet eye, but with lines of slender strength.

"When I told them I wanted a man big enough and tough enough to tackle a grizzly," he said, "they sent me to you."

"How much?" I said. "And where's the grizzly?"

"His name is Henry Wetterling, and he's the boss of Battle Basin. And I'll give you a thousand dollars."

"What do I do?"

"There's a girl up there, and her name is Nana Maduro. She owns a ranch on Cherry Creek. Wetterling wants the girl, and he wants the ranch. I don't want him to have either."

"You want him dead?"

"I want him out of there. Use your own judgment. When I hire a man for a job, I don't tell him how to do it." This man with the scholar's face was more than a quiet man; he could be a hard man.

"All right," I said.

"One thing more" — he smiled a little, quietly, as though enjoying what he was about to say — "Wetterling is top dog and he walks a wide path, but he has two men to back him." He smiled again. "Their names are Clevenger and Mack."

The bartender brought a lemon and salt, and I drank my tequila.

"The answer is still the same," I told him, then, "but the price is higher. I want five thousand dollars."

His expression did not change, but he reached in his pocket and drew out a wallet and counted green bills on the dirty table. He counted two thousand dollars.

"I like a man who puts the proper estimate on a job," he said. "The rest when you're finished."

He pushed back his chair and got up, and I looked at the green bills and thought of the long months of punching cows I'd have to put in to earn that much — if anybody, anywhere, would give me a job.

"Where do you fit in?" I asked. "Do you want the girl or the ranch or Wetterling's hide?"

"You're paid," he said pointedly, "for a job. Not for questions. . . ."

There was sunlight on the trail, and cloud shadows on the hills, and there was a time of riding, and a time of resting, and an afternoon, hot and still like cyclone weather when I walked my big red horse down the dusty street of the town of Battle Basin.

They looked at me, the men along the street, and well they could look. I weighed two hundred and forty pounds, but looked twenty-five pounds lighter. I was three inches over six feet, with black hair curling around my ears under a black flat-brimmed, flat-crowned hat, and the brim was dusty and the crown was torn. The shirt I wore was dark red, under a black horsehide vest, and there was a scar on my left cheek where a knife blade had bit to the bone. The man who had owned that knife left his bones in a pack rat's nest down Sonora way.

My boots were run-down at the heels and my jeans were worn under the chaps stained almost black. And when I swung down, men gathered around to look at my horse. Big Red is seventeen hands high and weighs thirteen hundred pounds — a blood bay with black mane, tail, and fore-lock.

"That's a lot of horse," a man in a white apron said. "It takes a man to ride a stallion."

"I ride him," I said, and walked past them into the bar. The man in the white apron followed me. "I drink tequila," I said.

He brought out a bottle and opened it, then found lemon and salt. So I had a drink there, and another, and looked around the room, and it all looked familiar. For there had been a time —

"I'm looking for a ranch," I said, "on Cherry Creek. It's owned by Nana Maduro."

The bartender's face changed before my eyes

149

and he mopped the bar. "See Wetterling," he said. "He hires for them."

"I'll see the owner," I said, and put down my glass.

A girl was coming up the street, walking fast. She had flame-red hair and brown eyes. When she saw Big Red she stopped dead still. And I stood under the awning and rolled a cigarette and watched her, and knew what she was feeling.

She looked around at the men. "I want to buy that horse," she said. "Who owns him?"

A man jerked a thumb at me, and she looked at me and took a step closer. I saw her lips part a little and her eyes widen.

She was all woman, that one, and she had it where it showed. And she wore her sex like a badge, a flaunting and a challenge — the way I liked it.

"You own this horse?"

One step took me out of the shade and into the sun, a cigarette in my lips. I'm a swarthy man, and her skin was golden and smooth, despite the desert sun.

"Hello, Lou," she said. "Hello, Lou Morgan."

"This is a long way from Mazatlán," I said. "You were lovely then, too."

"You were on the island," she said, "a prisoner. I thought you were still there."

"I was remembering you, and no walls could hold me," I said, smiling a little, "so I found a way out and away. The prison will recover in time."

"How did you know I was here?"

"I didn't," I said. "Remember? I killed a man for you and you left me, with never a word or a line. You left me like dirt in the street."

And when that was said I walked by her and stepped into saddle. I looked down at her and said, "You haven't changed. Under that fine-lady manner you're still a tramp."

A big young man who stood on the walk filled with the pride of his youth, thought he should speak. So I jumped the stallion toward him, and when we swept abreast I grabbed him by his shirtfront.

I swung him from his feet and muscled him up, half strangling, and held him there at eye level, my arm bent to hold him, my knuckles under his chin.

"That was a private conversation," I said. "The lady and I understand each other."

Then I slapped him, booming slaps that left his face white and the mark of my hand there, and I let him drop. My horse walked away and took a trail out of town.

But those slaps had been good for my soul, venting some of the fury I was feeling for her! Not the fury of anger, although there was that, too, but the fury of man-feeling rising within me, the great physical need I had for that woman that stirred me and gripped me and made my jaws clench and my teeth grind.

Nana Maduro! And that thin-faced man in the cantina hiring me to come and get you away from

151

this — what was his name? — Wetterling!

Nana Maduro, who was Irish and Spanish and whom I had loved and wanted when I was seventeen, and for whom I had killed a man and been sentenced to hang. Only the man I killed had been a dangerous man, a powerful man in Mexico, and feared, and not all were sorry that he had died. These had helped me, had got my sentence commuted to life imprisonment, and after two years I broke out and fled to the hills, and after two more years word had come that the records had been lost and that I was a free man.

At fifteen Nana Maduro had been a woman in body and feeling, but untried yet and restless because of it.

And at seventeen I had been raw and powerful, a seasoned Indian fighter knowing mining, hunting, and riding, but a boy in emotion and temper.

It was different now that seven years had passed. Nana now was full-flowered and gorgeous. But they had been seven hard, lean years for me, a man who rode with a gun and rode alone, a man who fought for pay, with a gun for hire.

Three days I rode the hills and saw no man, but looked upon the country through eyes and field glasses. And I saw much, and understood much.

Cherry Creek range was dream range, knee-deep to a tall steer with waving grass and flowers of the prairie. Even on the more barren stretches there were miles of antelope bush and sheep fat, the dry-looking desert plants rich in food for cattle. There was water there, so the cattle need walk but little and could keep their flesh, and there was shade from the midday sun.

And this belonged to Nana Maduro, to Nana, whom I'd loved as a boy, and desired as a man. And did I love as a man? Who could say?

She had cattle by the thousand on her rolling hills, and a ranch house like none I had ever seen, low and lovely and shaded, a place for a man to live. And a brand, N M, and a neighbor named Wetterling.

The Wetterling ranch was north and west of hers, but fenced by a range of hills, high-ridged and not to be crossed by cattle, and beyond the ridge the grass was sparse and there were few trees. A good ranch as such ranches go, but not the rolling, grass-waving beauty of Cherry Creek.

Then I saw them together. He was a huge man, bigger than I was, blond and mighty. At least two inches taller than I, and heavier, but solid. He moved light on his feet and quickly, and he could handle a horse.

Other things I saw. Nana was without friends. She was hemmed in by this man, surrounded by him. People avoided her through fear of him, until she was trapped, isolated. It could be a plan to win her finally, or to take her ranch if the winning failed.

But they laughed together and raced together, and they rode upon the hills together. And on the night of the dance in Battle Basin, they came to it together.

For that night I was shaved clean and dusted, my boots were polished, and though I went to the dance and looked at the girls, there was only one woman in that room for me.

She stood there with her big man, and I started toward her across the floor, my big California spurs jingling. I saw her face go white to the lips and saw her start to speak, and then I walked by her and asked the daughter of a rancher named Greenway for a dance.

As the Greenway girl and I turned away in the waltz I saw Nana's face again, flaming red, then white, her fine eyes blazing. So I danced with Ann Greenway, and I danced with Rosa McQueen, and I danced with the girls of the village and from the ranches, but I did not dance with Nana Maduro.

Nana watched me. That I saw. She was angry, too, and that I had expected, for when does the hunter like for the deer to escape? Especially, the wounded deer?

Two men came in when the evening was half gone, one of them a thin man with a sickly face and a head from which half the hair was gone, and in its place a scar. This was Clevenger. His partner Mack was stocky and bowlegged and red of face.

Both wore their guns tied down, and both were dangerous. They were known along the border for the men they had killed. They were feared men who had not acquired their reputations without reason.

They were there when I stopped not far away from where Wetterling was talking to Nana. I saw Wetterling move toward her as if to take her for a dance, and I moved quickly, saying, "Will you dance?" and wheeled her away as I spoke.

Wetterling's face was dark and ugly, and I saw the eyes of his two killers upon me, but I held Nana close, and good she felt in my arms. And she looked up at me, her lips red and soft and wet, and her eyes blazing.

"Let me go, you fool! They'll kill you for this!"

"Will they now?" I smiled at her, but my heart was pounding and my lips were dry, and my being was filled with the need of her. "You'll remember that was tried once, long ago."

Then I held her closer, her breasts tight against me, my arm about her slim waist, our bodies moving in the dance.

"To die for this," I said, "would not be to die in vain."

It was my mother's family that spoke, I think, for poetic as the Welsh may be, and my father was Welsh, it is the Spanish who speak of dying for love, though they are never so impractical. My mother's name was Ibañez.

When the dance was finished, Nana pulled away from me. "Leave me here," she said, and then when I took her arm to return her to Wetterling, she begged, "Please, Lou!"

My ears were deaf. So I took her to him and stopped before him, and, with his two trained dogs close by, I said, "She dances beautifully, my friend, and better with me than with you — and what are you trying to do with that fresh cut trail through the woods? Get your cattle onto her grass?"

Then I turned my back and walked away and the devil within me feeling the glory of having stirred the man to fury, wanting that, yet desolate to be leaving her. For now I knew I loved Nana Maduro. Not prison nor time nor years nor her coldness had killed it. I still loved her.

At the door as I left, a red-faced man with bowed legs who stood there said, "You've a fine horse and it's a nice night to ride. Cross the

156

Territory line before you stop."

"See you tomorrow," I said.

"Have a gun in your hand, if you do," he said to me, and went back inside. Mack, a brave man.

In the morning I rode the hills again, doing a sight of thinking. Wetterling wanted both the ranch and the girl, and no doubt one as much as the other. Another man wanted the place, too, and maybe the girl. But why that particular ranch?

Lovely, yes. Rich with grass, yes. But considering the obstacles and the expense — why? Hatred? It could be. A man can hate enough. But my employer was not a hating man, to my thinking. He just knew what he wanted, and how to get it.

Small ranchers and riders with whom I talked could give me no clue. I did not ask outright if they knew my employer, but I could tell they must know the man.

The trail I had found through the woods was guarded now. Two men loafed near the N M side of it, both with rifles across their knees. Through my glasses I studied that trail. It was wide, and it was well cut. When I got into my saddle I saw something else — a gleam of sunlight reflecting on a distant mountainside. Distant, but still on Maduro range.

Big Red took to the trail and I rode for so long that it was after dark before I returned to Battle Basin. I left Big Red stabled in a small, outlying two-horse barn, and, with my guns on, I walked down into town. I moved quietly among the buildings until I reached the street. Merging with the shadows I looked to right and left.

A drunk cowhand staggered along the boardwalk across the street. He lurched against a building, then went on. Starting to step out into the light I froze, for it suddenly had come to me that the drunken cowhand had not been talking to himself, but had spoken to someone in the shadows!

Moving back into the darkness I worked my way along in the shadows toward the corral. There were horses there, saddled, bridled, and tied — an even dozen of them, all wearing the Wetterling brand. I traced it with my finger.

In another hour I knew the Wetterling crew would be all over the town, in ambush, waiting for me. No matter where I showed up, they would have me in a cross fire. There had been some good planning done! They were figuring I'd spoil their beautiful plan and were out to stop me, but they'd forgotten the life I'd lived, and how I'd lived the years I had only through caution. I was an Indian on my feet, quiet and easy.

From the cover of the darkness, I studied the saloon, the roofs of the town. And then I walked up to the back door of the saloon and went in.

Mack was there, at the bar with another man, not Clevenger. One man could be deadly, two were poison, but as I entered I said, "All right, Mack. You looking for me?"

It startled him. I saw his shoulders bunch, then

he turned. I was standing half in the shadows, and it was not right for him. His partner was more foolish. The instant he saw me he grabbed for a gun.

Two guns were on my hips, but I had another in a shoulder holster, a Wes Hardin rig. When both moved for their guns, I shucked it.

Strange how at times like that minutes seem hours, and the seconds are expanded unbelievably. Mack's gun was coming up fast, faster by far than that of the other man. In the background the bartender was transfixed, his mouth gaping, eyes bulging. Another man who had started through the door and was directly in the line of fire stood there, frozen, and in that instant the room was deathly still.

My shoulder gun slid true and easy. My hand rolled outward as I brought my elbow down, and the gun jumped in my hand. The flash from Mack's gun came a breath later. I saw him bunch his shoulders forward as if he'd been struck in the stomach, then my gun muzzle had moved left and the gun bucked again.

Mack's companion pulled his feet together, went up to tiptoes and fell. Mack caught himself on the table corner and stared at me, aware that I'd killed him. With that awful realization in his eyes, his gun fell.

Then I was out the back door, going up the outside stairs, running lightly and through the door, ducking into the first room, luckily empty. I climbed out the window, stood up on the sill and, catching the roof edge, pulled myself up and over.

Men rushed by between the buildings, footsteps pounded in the hallways below. The chase was in full cry. Lying there, stone still, I waited.

Movement in the room below alerted me. Then voices spoke, near the window, and I could hear every word plainly.

"You knew him before?" That would be Wetterling.

"In Mexico," Nana's voice answered. "He rode for my father, and when Sanchez killed my father and took me away with him, Lou Morgan followed. He killed Sanchez in the street, then took me home. He was tried for it and sent to prison."

"You love him?"

"Love him?" Her voice was careless. "How could I? I was a child, and he was a boy, and we scarcely knew each other. And I don't know him now."

"You've been different since he came."

"And you've been insistent." Nana's voice was edged. "I'm not sure which it is you really want — my ranch or me."

He evidently started toward her, for I heard her move back. "No!"

"But you told me you'd marry me."

"I said I might." She was right at the window now. "Now go away and find some more gunmen. You'll need them."

He started to protest, but she insisted. I heard the door close then, and I heard Nana humming.

She came to the window and said distinctly:

"Next time you use my window for a ladder, please clean your boots."

Swinging down by the edge of the roof, I went through the window and away from it.

She was wearing a blue riding outfit, her hair beautifully done. I've never seen a girl look more desirable. She saw it in my eyes, for I was making no effort to conceal what I felt.

"What are you, Lou?" she demanded. "An animal?"

"Sometimes."

My blood was heavy in my pulse. I could feel it throb, and I stood there, feet apart, knowing myself for what I was — a big, dark man hunted in the night, looking at a woman for whom a man would give his soul.

"When I'm close to you I am," I added.

"Is that a nice thing to say?"

"Maybe not. But you like it."

"You presume too much."

I sat down, watching her. I knew that the amusement which must be in my eyes bothered her. She knew how to handle men and she was used to doing that. She had been able to handle me, once. That was long ago. I'd left tracks over a lot of country since then.

"You're not safe here," she said. "Twenty men are hunting you. You should go — ride on out of here."

"Know a man with thin hair, nice-looking, like a college professor?"

The question startled her, but the sharpening of her attention told me she did. "Why do you ask?" she said.

"He hired me to come here. To stop Wetterling."

"You *lie!*"

It flashed at me, a stabbing, bitter word.

An angry word.

"It's true."

She studied me.

"Then you didn't come because I was in trouble?"

"How could I? How could I know?" I smiled. "But the idea of a job to keep a man away from you was attractive. I liked the idea."

Despite her wish not to show it, she was disappointed. She had been seeing me as a knight-errant, come to her rescue. As if she needed it! Most men were toys for her. Yet she did need rescue, more than she guessed.

It was not Wetterling who made me jealous now, but the unknown man, my employer.

"He would not do such a thing," she insisted. "Besides, he doesn't even know about — about Henry."

"He knows. That isn't all he knows. He's after your ranch, too, you know."

She was wicked now. "Oh, you liar! You contemptible liar! He's not even interested in ranching! He's never been on a ranch! He wouldn't think of hiring a — *a killer!*"

The name had been applied before. To an

extent, it was true. I shoved my battered hat back on my head and began to build a smoke, taking my time.

"Wetterling doesn't care about the ranch, either," I said slowly. "He's interested in only part of it."

It went against the grain for her to believe that any man was interested in anything but her. Yet she accepted the accusation against Wetterling, but against the other man, no.

That was why the other man bothered me most.

"I don't know what you mean," she said.

"Nana Maduro," I said thoughtfully. "It's a lovely name. An old name. So old there was a Maduro among the first to come to New Spain. He had a brother who was a Jesuit."

"There were Jesuits in your family, too."

"How'd you come to buy that ranch? Because of your grandfather, wasn't it? He left you the money and told you to buy it? That if you did you'd never want?"

She was genuinely puzzled.

"And so?"

Sitting with my big forearms on the back of the chair I straddled, I could see somebody down below, between the buildings. I lit my cigarette and inhaled, tensing slightly.

"Have you forgotten the old stories?" I asked. "Of the *conducta?*"

She paled a little. "But that was just a story!"

"Was it? Your grandfather insisted on this

place. Why? When it was so far from all you knew?"

"You mean — it's on *this* place? *My* place?"

"Why do you think they want it?" I shrugged. I heard a boot grate on gravel and got up, keeping back from the window. "Wetterling, and your scholarly friend?"

"That's ridiculous! How would they know? How could *he* know?"

I moved toward the door, but stopped suddenly. "So beautiful!" I said softly. "Little peasant."

Her face flamed. "You — *you* call *me*, a Maduro, a peasant! Why, you —"

My smile was wide. "A Maduro was a mule driver in the expedition. My ancestor was its *capitán!*"

Ducking out the door before Nana could throw something, I glanced quickly up and down the hall, then swiftly stepped back through. Before she realized what was happening I had an arm about her. I drew her quickly to me. She started to fight, but what are blows? I kissed her and, liking it, kissed her again. Was I mistaken or was there a return of the kiss?

Then I let her go and stepped quickly out and shut the door. "Coward!" I heard her say, as I ran lightly down the hall.

Then they were coming. I heard them coming up the back stairs, coming up the front stairs. I dodged into the nearest room, put down my cigarette and dropped two more cigarette papers upon the glowing end; then, ripping a blanket from a bed, I touched the end to it. Instantly, it flared up.

Quickly I crossed the room. The fire would give me only a moment of time before they put it out. I was at the window when I heard a yell as somebody smelled smoke.

"Fire!"

Running steps in the hall outside, then stamping feet. Glancing out the window, I saw only one man below. He had turned his head slightly. Swinging from the window, I dropped the eighteen feet to the ground.

He wheeled, swinging up his rifle, and I grabbed the barrel end and jerked it toward me. Off balance, he fell forward. On one knee I grasped his shirt and crotch and heaved him over my head and into the wall. Then I was up and running.

A shot slammed at me. I grabbed the top pole of the corral and dropped over it. Horses scattered. Running to the gate I ripped it open and, swinging into a saddle, lay far down on the other side of the horse I had grabbed as we came out together. All the horses in a mad rush, and me among them.

Shots rang out, curses, yells. The horses charged down the alley. A guard tried to leap aside, almost made it, then we were racing on. Swinging the horse I rode from the crush, I headed for the stable where Big Red was waiting.

Dropping from the horse, I had started forward when, too late, I saw them waiting there — three men with guns. I felt a violent blow, my leg went from under me, thunder broke around in a wave, and then — pure instinct did it — my guns were shooting, shooting again.

Then somehow the men were gone and I was in the saddle on Big Red, and we were off and running and there was — odd, so close to town — the smell of pines. . . .

Only it was not close to town when the pine smell came to me. The pines were on a far mountain, and I was on the ground. Not far from me

Big Red was feeding. Rolling over, I sat up, and the movement started me bleeding again. My head throbbed and a wave of pain went through me. I lay back on the grass and stared up at the sky where clouds gathered.

After a while I tried again, and got up to the stream which had attracted Big Red. I drank, and drank again. Under the low clouds I ripped my jeans and examined my wounds. Then I bathed and dressed them as best I could, thankful that I knew the ways of the Indians and the plants they used in cases like this.

Back in my saddle I rode deeper into the hills. Far behind and below me was the ranch, but I kept riding, looking for a rock shaped like the back of a head. Twice I stopped to look back. Riders were spread across the country below, searching for me.

A spatter of rain came. It felt cool against my face. Lightning darted, thunder crashed. Feebly I struggled into my slicker. Humped against the pound of the rain, I went on.

The rain would wash out my tracks. I would be safe. Big Red plodded on, and thunder rolled and tumbled among the great peaks, and once an avalanche of rocks roared down ahead of us, but we kept on. And then in a sharp streak of lightning, I saw the head!

Rounding it, I rode right into the tumbled boulders, weaving my way among them. Twice I ran into blind alleys. And then, after retracing my steps, I found the right one and a way opened before me.

Trees, their blank trunks like bars of iron through the steel net of the rain. My body loose in the saddle, somehow guiding the red horse. A dip downward, a mountain valley, a steep trail. Then grass, water, trees — and the arched door of an ancient Spanish mission!

In an adobe house we took shelter, Big Red and I. From *amolillo* and maize I made a poultice for my wounds and rested there, eating only a little at a time from the jerked beef and bread in my saddlebags.

Here I slept, awakened, changed the poultice on my wounds, then slept again.

I would be safe here. No one had found this place in two hundred years, and no one was likely to find it now. And then night came and the wind howled and there was a long time when the rain beat upon the ancient roof, leaking in at places and running along the ancient floor.

There was a long time when there was only lightning, thunder, and the wind. Then came a time when hands seemed to touch me and caress me, and I dreamed that I was not dead and that the lips of my loved one were on mine again.

Morning came and I was awake. Sunlight fell through the ancient door. Outside, I could hear Big Red cropping grass, and his saddle and bridle were in the corner. I could not even remember taking them off.

My head was on a pillow of grass, and a blanket covered me. My wound would need care and I rolled over and sat up. But I saw then that the dressing was fresh and of white cloth that I had never seen before. There were ghosts in this place.

And then I heard someone singing, and a shadow was in the door, and then Nana came through it, bearing an armful of flowers.

She stopped when she saw I was awake.

"So," I said, "you came."

"Who else would come? Who else could find you?"

"You told no one?"

"Not anyone at all."

She came over to me, remaining a respectful distance away because despite my illness there was a hunger in my eyes when I looked at her.

"I'm going back now," she said. "You must rest. I brought food, so there is plenty. Rest, recuperate, then ride away."

"Away?"

"Wetterling has hunted you like a wild animal. He will not listen. You killed Mack. You killed two other men and wounded several. He is determined to hunt you down."

Then I told her quietly and honestly that I would not ride away, that I would stay there, that her kisses were so rich they had spoiled me for other kisses. I must remain.

She was furious. She told me I was a fool. That she had never kissed me, would never let me kiss her again, that I must go away. She did not want me dead.

"You love me?"

"No!" she spat at me. "Love you? A killer? A hired gunfighter? A no-good? Go away! I just don't want you dead after what you did for me long ago."

Sadly I shook my head. "But if I am gone I will not be able to make love to you. That is bad."

She got up, holding her chin high. It was lovely to see her like that, but she went away and left me. . . .

Days passed into a week, and a week into another. I walked, I snared game. I ate what food was left. I searched the old mine, looked about. I found a place under the floor where —

I heard them coming too late. My guns were across the room.

It was my employer, and he was not alone. With him were two Yaqui Indians. Two of the wild ones. They all had guns and they were definite with them.

"I did not know," he said, "that you are an Ibañez."

"How did you get here?"

"Watched Nana. It was simple. You vanished. You had to be somewhere. What more likely place than here? So I watched her, for if anyone knew, she would. And now I have you."

He sat down. The Yaquis did not. "You failed in your job. Now tell me where the silver was buried, and the mission vessels."

"Who knows?"

170

His smile was not nice. "You have heard of pinning needles of pitch pine through the skin and lighting them? The Yaquis understand that sort of thing. That is the way we will start unless you talk."

It was a bad way to die. And I was not ready for it. Yet how strong was I? How much recovered?

"We might make a bargain."

"Only one. I'll give you your life if you tell me."

Of course, he lied. The cold ones are the dangerous ones. He would kill me when he had picked the meat from the shell of my story. It was better to die. "All right," I said. "I'm not anxious to die."

He would be difficult to fool, this one. Wetterling would have been easier. I looked at my hand upon my knee. How much of my strength had I lost? How much of my agility? During the snaring of game, the walking, the searching, my strength had seemed to come back, but two weeks was not much, and I had lost blood.

"It is late," I told him, "for we need the morning sun."

He frowned. "Why? This is the place."

My shrug was tolerant. "Here? Such an obvious place? How could they know it would not be found? The trail was good then. No, the silver is not here, nor are the vessels."

Reluctantly, he listened. More reluctantly, they began to bring in blankets and food for the night.

They allowed me to help with the fire, and I remembered Nana saying that Wetterling was searching for me feverishly. His men were scouring the country. I thought of that, and of the fire.

It was late afternoon, an hour before darkness. The air was still. Moving slowly, to make them think my strength had not yet returned, I helped gather wood.

So you know the *ocotillo?* Candlewood, it is called. A rare and wonderful plant. Not a cactus, although it is thorny, its stems are straight like canes, and it blossoms with brilliant flowers of scarlet.

We of the desert know it also as strong with resin, gum, and wax, that it burns brightly, fiercely, and has still another quality also.

Rarely does One find a dead *ocotillo.* This plant knows the secret of life. Yet sometimes single canes die, or sometimes one is broken off, or blown down by winds. There was a dead one near, uprooted in a slide. Gathering fuel, I gathered it. Helping to build the fire, I added the *ocotillo.* The Yaquis were not watching, and Borneman, for that was my employer's name, did not know the *ocotillo.* And we were inside the building.

On the fire it crackled, fierce tongues of flame ran along the canes, the fire burned high, and up the fireplace went billows of intensely black smoke!

IV

We ate well that night, for Borneman traveled well. He had plenty of blankets, for he was a man who liked comfort. As who does not? But there are times and times.

They bound me well. He did not trust the Yaquis to do that. Not Borneman. He bound me himself and the Yaquis could have done it better. A blanket was thrown over me, and soon I heard them breathing regularly in sleep. Borneman and I slept near the fireplace. The Yaquis were near the door.

Large as I am, I am nimble, and my insides are resilient. And there was a trick I knew. My wrists were bound behind my back, but by spreading my arms as wide as possible, I backed my hips through them. Like most riding men, my hips are narrow, but it still was a struggle. I got through, though; then drawing my knees high under my chin, I brought my bound hands under my feet so they were in front of me. My teeth worried the knots until they were loose. Two hours it took me, and careful work.

Then I was free. The breathing of my captors was still even, regular. In my blanket I got to my feet and, like a cat, moved to the door. As I moved to the open space a Yaqui's breathing broke. I heard a muffled gasp, and he started to rise. But my right fingers quickly had his throat

173

and my left sank into his wind. He was slippery, like a snake, but I had him off the floor.

He struggled desperately, silently, but my hand remained at his throat and the struggles grew weaker. I took him outside, dropping his body like carrion where they would find it. A killer he was, one who would have tortured me. I felt no regret.

And then I fled — into the trees and to the grassy park where Big Red was concealed. With a hackamore made of the ropes they had used to bind me, I bridled him. My saddle was back there, but I had ridden bareback many a time. I crawled upon him, and rode into the darkness of the night.

After awhile, I heard riders and held myself from the path with a hand at my horse's nostrils until they were by. One was a huge man. Wetterling. They had seen the smoke then.

A gun! I must have a gun.

Big Red ran like the wind, and I loved his easy movements. He ran and ran, and when day was not yet gray in the eastern sky, I was riding into the trees near the ranch house of Nana Maduro. Was she here, or in the hotel room above the saloon?

In the last of the darkness I found her window, heard her breathing inside, and put a leg through, then another. I touched her arms, and her eyes opened. Her head turned.

She did not cry out, but she sat up quickly. It was enough to take a man's breath.

"Lou Morgan!" she exclaimed in a startled whisper. "What are you doing here?"

"I'll need a gun," I said, "or better, a pair of guns. Your lovers are snarling at each other at the mission where you left me."

Then I told her of the pitch slivers and the Yaqui. At first her eyes were hot with disbelief, but gradually changed to doubt. Then I told her of the *ocotillo* smoke that had brought Wetterling, and I laughed at my enemies.

She dressed swiftly while I watched out the window and saw dawn throw crimson arrows into the sky. Out in the cool halls of her house she took me and got a pair of pistols, ornamented, beautiful — two Russian .44s, a pistol made by Smith & Wesson. A masterpiece!

With these belted on, plus a Winchester .76 and a belt of ammunition, I was ready.

With her own hands she quickly made breakfast. I drank black coffee, and ate eggs and ham, and looked upon her grace and beauty, and forgot. Until too late.

We heard them come. From the window we saw them. A half-dozen horsemen, one with a bandaged head, one with an arm in a sling, and three horses with empty saddles. But Wetterling and Borneman were riding together, side by side. My enemies had joined hands.

What to do?

It had to be quickly, and it had to be now. These men were conscienceless. They would kill Nana Maduro as soon as they would kill me, and if they forced from us the secret of the mission gold and silver, then we would die.

Into the gray of morning I stepped, and saw the blood of dawn on their faces. My rifle stood by the door, my two guns lay against my thighs.

"Good morning," I said. "The thieves ride together."

Wetterling's eyes were ugly, but those of Borneman were only cold. I made up my mind then — Borneman must die. He was too cool, with his scholar's face and his quiet voice, and his thin, cruel lips.

"Let's be reasonable," he said quietly. "You and Nana are alone here, except for two riders who are old men, and even they have gone to a line camp. Your Indian woman cook is as helpless as you. Tell us where the gold is and we'll leave."

"We'll tell you nothing!" I said.

"He speaks for me," Nana said. "I hope he always speaks for me. And to think I had always believed you — a famous scientist my grandfather called you — were his friend!"

Wetterling's hatred was obvious. He still wanted Nana. "I'll change you!" he said. "I'll break you!"

"With the gold," Borneman said, "you can buy fifty women."

There was a silence then, while a quail called. Silence while dawn made a glory of the sky; and the dark pines fringed against the hills; and the air was cool and good.

Six men, and one of them Clevenger, whose partner I had killed. One of them a Yaqui, hating me. And a girl behind me whom they would not spare even if I died, and whom I knew would suffer the tortures of hell before she'd die, for she had courage, and would not tell.

That decided me. Numbers give courage, but they give it to the enemy, too. They gave it to me. Six men, and growing in me a terrible rage and a terrible fear. A rage against them, and a fear for her, for Nana Maduro whom I had loved since she was a child on her father's ranch.

"You want gold and you've come prepared to buy it," I said, "with your blood." I took a step forward. "The price will be high, my friends, and Borneman, you will owe me, in a few minutes, the five thousand you offered me to kill Wetterling."

Wetterling's big blond head snapped around. *"What?"* he barked. "You paid him to kill me? Why, you —"

He struck at Borneman and my guns came up shooting. As he struck, his horse swung broadside, cutting off a rider whose gun came up fast. That gave me an instant I desperately needed. Three men were out of the picture, but I saw Clevenger's eyes blazing and shot into them. His scarred head seemed to blast apart as he slid from his horse. Behind me the Winchester barked and another rider was knocked from the saddle, not dead, but hurt.

The Yaqui slammed his heels into his mount

and charged me, and I stepped aside, grabbed his arm, and like a cat was in the saddle behind him with a left forearm like a bar of iron across his throat. The plunging horse swung wide and, with the Yaqui's body for shield, I shot again and again.

Wetterling's horse went down and he was thrown free. Borneman hit the ground and rolled. I threw a quick shot at him and sand splashed his face and into his eyes. He screamed and clawed at his face, then the Yaqui twisted and I felt a knife blade rip my hide. With a great effort I tore him free of me and threw him to the ground. He started up, but the plunging, bucking horse was over him and his scream was drowned in the sound of the Winchester.

I hit the ground, guns empty. Borneman still pawed at his eyes. Clevenger was down and dead. Wetterling was getting to his feet. Another rider was sprawled dead or injured, and still another clutched a broken arm and swore.

Wetterling looked at me and shook himself, then started for me. Suddenly I felt the fires of hell in my blood and I swung for his chin.

It missed. He came in low and hard, grappling me about the hips, so instead of resisting, I went back quickly and the force of his tackle and my lack of resistance carried him past and over me.

On our feet, we walked toward each other. I feinted, he stepped in, and I hit him with a right that jarred him to his heels. He swung, and then we walked in, punching with both hands.

It was a shindig! A glorious shindig! He swung low and missed me, and I brought my knee into his face. His nose crushed to pulp and I hit him with both hands as he straightened back. He fell, and I walked close. As he started to get up I slugged him again.

My wounded leg was burning like fire, my breath was coming in gasps, my head felt dizzy. Somehow he got up. He hit me again and again, but then I got him by the throat and crotch and threw him to the ground. He started up and I hit him. Blood splashed from his broken nose and he screamed. I hit him again, and he blubbered.

Then I walked back to Nana. "If he moves," I said, "shoot him. I'm going to sit down. . . ."

If you should, in the passing of years, come to the ranch on Cherry Creek, look for the N M brand. You'll find us there. I've tequila in the cupboard and brandy on the shelf, but if you want women, you'll have to bring your own, for Nana's mine, and we're watching the years together.

The gold we gave to the church, the silver to charity, and the jewels we kept for ourselves.

My hair is grizzled now, gray, and I'm heavier by the years, but Nana Maduro Morgan says I'm as good a man as I ever was.

And Nana should know.

RIDE OR
START SHOOTIN'

Chapter 1
The Bet

Tollefson saw the horses grazing in the creek bottom and pulled up sharply. "Harry," his voice was harsh and demanding as always, "whose horses are those?"

"Some drifter name of Tandy Meadows. He's got some fine-lookin' stock there."

"He's passin' through?"

"Well," Harry Fulton's reluctance sprang from his knowledge of Art Tollefson's temper, "he says he aims to run a horse in the quarter races."

Surprisingly, Tollefson smiled. "Oh, he does, does he? Too bad he hasn't money. I'd like to take it away from him if he had anything to run against Lady Luck."

Passman had his hat shoved back on his head. It was one of those wide-across-the-cheekbones faces with small eyes, a blunt jaw, and hollow cheeks. Everybody west of Cimarron knew Tom Passman for a gunfighter, and knew that Passman had carried the banner of Art Tollefson's legions into the high-grass country.

Ranching men had resented their coming with the big Flying T outfit and thirty thousand head of stock. Passman accepted their resentment and told them what they could do. Two, being plainsmen, elected to try it. Harry Fulton had helped to dig their graves.

It was Passman who spoke now. "He's got some real horses, boss."

Tollefson's coveting eyes had been appreciating that. It was obvious that whoever this drifter was, he knew horseflesh. In the twenty-odd head there were some splendid animals. For an instant a shadow of doubt touched him. Such a string might carry a quarter horse faster than Lady Luck. But the doubt was momentary, for his knowledge of the Lady and his pride of possession would not leave room for that. Lady Luck had bloodlines. She was more than range stock.

"Let's go talk to him," he said, and reined his bay around the start down the slope toward the creek.

Within view there was a covered wagon and there were two saddled horses. As they rode down the slope, a man stepped from behind the wagon to meet them. He was a short, powerfully setup Negro with one ear missing and the other carrying a small gold ring in the lobe. His boots were down at heel and his jeans worn.

"Howdy!" Tollefson glanced around. "Who is the owner here?" The tone was suited to an emperor, and behind the wall of his armed riders, Tollefson was almost that. Yet there is something about ruling that fades the perspective, denying clarity to the mind.

"I'm the owner."

The voice came from behind them and

184

Tollefson felt sudden anger. Fulton, who was not a ruler and hence had an unblunted perspective, turned his head with the thought that whoever this man was, he was cautious, and no fool.

As they came down the hill the Negro emerged just at the right time to focus all their eyes, and then the other man appeared from behind them. It was the trick of a magician, of a man who understands indirection.

Tollefson turned in his saddle, and Fulton saw the quick shadow on Tom Passman's face, for Passman was not a man who could afford to be surprised.

A tall man stood at the edge of the willows. A man whose face was shadowed by the brim of a flat-crowned gray hat, worn and battered. A bullet, Fulton noticed, had creased the crown, neatly notching the edge, and idly he wondered what had become of the man who fired that shot.

The newcomer wore a buckskin vest but had no gun in sight. His spurs were large roweled, California style, and in his hand he carried a rawhide riata. This was grass-rope country, and forty-five feet was a good length, yet from the look of this rope it was sixty or more.

"You the owner?" Tollefson was abrupt as always. "I hear you're plannin' to race a quarter horse against my Lady Luck."

"Aim to." The man came forward, moving with the step of a woodsman rather than a rider.

"I'm Tollefson. If you have any money and want to bet, I'm your man. If you don't have money, maybe we could bet some stock."

Tandy Meadows pushed back his hat from his strong bronzed face, calm with that assurance that springs from inner strength. Not flamboyant strength, nor pugnacious, but that of a man who goes his own way and blazes his own trails.

"Yeah," Tandy said slowly, digging out the makings, "I've two or three quarter horses. I figured to run one of them. It isn't much point which of them." He scratched a match on his trouser leg. "What made you figure I had no money? I got a mite of change I aimed to bet."

Tollefson's smile was patronizing. "I'm talking about *money*, man! I like to bet! I was thinking," he paused for effect and he deliberately made his voice casual, "five thousand dollars."

"Five?" Meadows lifted an eyebrow. "Well, all right. I guess I can pick up a few more small bets around to make it interesting."

Tollefson's skin tightened over his cheekbones. He was no gambling man, but it built his ego to see men back up and hesitate at the thought of five thousand dollars in one bet. "What do you mean? You want to bet *more* than five thousand dollars?"

"Sort of figured it." Meadows drew deeply on his cigarette. "I heard there was a gambling man down here who liked to bet enough to make it interesting."

Tollefson was deeply affronted. Not many men could afford to bet that kind of money, and he liked to flaunt big bets and show them who they

186

were dealing with. Yet here was a man who calmly accepted his bet and hinted that it was pretty small potatoes. Somewhere in the group behind him he thought he detected a subdued snicker, and the casual indifference of this man Meadows irritated him.

"Whatever you want to put up," he snapped, "I'll cover! Name your price! I'll cover all you can get at two to one odds!"

"Now you're talkin'," Tandy said, sliding his thumbs behind his belt. "Aren't you the Tollefson from the Flying T? How about bettin' your ranch?"

Art Tollefson was shocked. He was profoundly shocked. This down-at-heels stranger offering to cover a bet against his *ranch!* Against the Flying T, sixty thousand head of stock and miles of rolling grassland, water holes, and buildings!

Lady Luck was his pride, a symbol of his power and money. She was the fastest thing he had ever seen on legs, and he liked to see her win. Yet his bets were merely for the sake of showing his large-handed way with money, of making him envied. At heart he was not a gambler and only put his money up reluctantly, but he was rarely called. Yet now he had been, and he knew that if he backed down now he would become the laughingstock of the range. It was a humiliation he neither wanted nor intended to endure.

"That's a rather large bet, my man," he said, for suddenly he realized the man must be bluffing. "Have you any idea what you're saying?

You'd have to show a lot of money to cover it."

Meadows smiled. It was the first flicker of expression that had come to his face, but the smile was pleasant. Yet there was a shadow beneath it that might have been faintly ironic. "What's the matter, Tollefson?" he taunted gently. "Gettin' chilly around the arches? Or were you bluffin' with that big money talk? Back down, if you like, and don't waste my time. I'll cover your little spread and more if need be, so put up or shut up."

Tollefson's fury broke. "Why, you impudent chump!" He stopped, his jaw setting hard. "All right, get on your horse and come to the bank with me! John Clevenger knows my ranch, and he knows horses! If you've got the collateral, you can put it up, and you've made a bet!"

Tandy swung astride one of the saddled horses. Tollefson's quick eyes saw the build of the animal. Arab, with a strain of Morgan by the look of it. If this horse was any evidence. . . . He shook off a momentary twinge of doubt.

Meadows turned his horse, then hesitated. "Don't you even want to see my horses? I've not decided which to run, but you're welcome to look 'em over."

"It's no matter!" Tollefson's fury was still riding him. He was bitter at the trap he had laid for himself. If this fool didn't have the money, why he would. . . . Just what he would do he wasn't sure but his face was flushed with angry blood.

188

Art Tollefson was not the only one who was feeling doubt. To Harry Fulton, who rode behind him, this seemed too pat to be an accident, and to Tom Passman it seemed the same way but with an added worry. Gifted at judging men, he knew Tandy Meadows should have been carrying a gun; yet there was none in sight, and it worried him.

Tandy Meadows looked straight down the road, aware that the crossroads of all his planning had been reached, and now everything depended on John Clevenger. He knew little about the banker except that the man was known and respected on the frontier, and that he was one of the original breeders of quarter horses. He was hard headed, yet a Western man to the very heels of his boots, and a man with the courage of his convictions. It was rumored of him that he had once accepted four aces in a poker game as collateral for a bank loan.

The bank at El Poleo was a low, gray stone building that looked like the fort it had to be to survive. Situated as it was, across the street from the Poleo Saloon, half the town saw Art Tollefson and the stranger draw up before the bank. It was in the nature of things that in a matter of minutes everyone in town knew what they had come for. The town was aghast.

Chapter 2
A Trap Closes

John Clevenger saw them coming with no idea of what they wanted. He had opened his bank against great odds and against even greater odds had kept it going. He had faith in his fellow man and his judgment of them, and was accustomed to the amazing ways of Western men. More than once he had loaned money on sheer courage and character. So far he had not lost by it.

Tollefson was a shrewd, hard-headed business man, yet one of overbearing manner who carried things with a high hand. Tollefson dealt in force and money power, Clevenger in character and self-respect. That Tollefson should make such a wager was beyond belief, yet Clevenger heard them out in silence.

"You have collateral for such a bet?" Clevenger asked. He studied Meadows thoughtfully and approved of what he saw.

Tandy drew a black leather case from his hip pocket and extracted a letter and some legal-appearing papers. Clevenger accepted them, started as if struck, then looked again and became very thoughtful. Twice he glanced up at Meadows. At last he got to his feet and pulled off his glasses. There was the ghost of a twinkle in his eyes as he studied Meadows. "I hardly know what to say, Mr. Meadows. I —" His voice faltered, then stopped.

"That's my collateral," Tandy said quietly. "I think you're the best judge. Tollefson seems to want a big bet on this race. I've called him. We came to see if you would accept this as collateral and put up the money to cover the bet." He glanced toward the flushed face of the rancher. "Of course, if he wants to welsh on the bet, now's his last chance."

"I'll be double slathered if I do!" Tollefson's fury was increased by his panic. He wanted nothing so much as to be safely out of this, but could see no escape without losing prestige, as important to him as life itself.

Clevenger stared thoughtfully at the papers. "Yes," he said at last, "I'll put up the money. Your bet's covered, Tollefson."

"Here — let me see that!" Tollefson's hand shot out, grabbing for the letter, but steely fingers caught his wrist.

Tandy Meadows jerked Tollefson's hand back and their eyes clashed. Half-blind with fury, Tollefson stared at the younger man. "Take your hands off me!" he shouted.

"Willingly," Meadows replied shortly, "only you have neither the need nor the right to touch those papers. Its contents are confidential. All you need is Clevenger's word that he will put up the money."

Stiffly, Tollefson drew back his hand, rubbing

191

his wrist. He stared hard at Meadows, genuinely worried now. Who was this man? Where did he get such money? What had so astonished Clevenger about the papers? And that grip! Why, his fingers were like a steel trap!

Abruptly, he turned and walked from the bank followed by Fulton and Tom Passman. Together they entered the saloon. Fulton rubbed his jaw nervously, wanting to talk to Tollefson. This was a crazy bet! The equivalent of a quarter of a million dollars on a quarter horse race against an unknown horse!

Of course, Lady Luck had consistently beaten all the horses that west Texas, New Mexico, and southern Colorado had found to race against the filly. There was no escaping the fact that she was fast. She was very fast.

"Boss," Fulton began hesitantly, "this bet ain't good sense. If I were you, I'd reconsider."

"You aren't me, so shut up!" Nobody needed to tell Tollefson that he had made a foolish bet. That was what pride could do for a man! The thought of withdrawing had rankled. He might have done it had Meadows not appeared so contemptuously sure he would. And in front of John Clevenger? The one man he had always failed to impress? Never!

He could just hear the laughter of the small ranchers whom he had forced back off their range. There was one thing he could not stand, and that was ridicule.

Outside the bank, Tandy Meadows stood and

stared thoughtfully up the street. Now he had done what he had started out to do, and it remained only to win. Tollefson had deliberately forced Jim Whitten from his water hole, giving him only the choice of giving up his ranch or dying. And Gene Bates was now slowly recovering from a bullet wound from Passman's gun. That had been the only time Tom Passman had drawn a gun at El Poleo that he failed to kill. His shot had been high, but he had walked away from Bates believing him dead.

Suddenly, Tandy saw a girl come from a store, then turn and start toward him. It was Janet Bates!

At the same moment, within the saloon, Art Tollefson saw Janet, and saw her walk up to Tandy holding out her hand! He downed his drink with a gulp. Who was this Tandy Meadows?

Tom Passman was leaning on the bar alongside of him and he turned his head slightly. It rankled Passman that Tandy Meadows had gotten behind him. He had always said that no man could without him knowing it. He lifted his glass and his cold eyes studied the liquor. "Boss," he whispered, "let me handle it."

Relief broke over Tollefson. Yes, that was the way. It was the best way, but not yet. Only as a last resort. It would be too obvious, altogether too obvious.

Anger hit him then. What was he worrying about? When had Lady Luck failed him? Why should he be afraid that she might now? After all, suppose she did win? The idea came to him that if she did, he would have twice as much money, and it gave him a sudden lift. And so easy, for Lady Luck was fast. She had never been beaten. She had never even had a hard fight to win. Her last quarter had been in twenty-three, and she had done equally well on at least two other occasions.

Janet Bates was staring up into Tandy's eyes. "Oh, Tandy! I was never so glad to see anyone in my life! But is it true? That you are going to race against Lady Luck?"

"Sure, I'm going to run Cholo Baby."

"Tandy, you mustn't! Dad says there isn't a horse in the country can touch Lady Luck."

"Your dad's a good cattleman, Janet, but he's never seen Cholo Baby. She's fast — fast enough to beat —" He stopped, then shrugged. "She's a runnin' little horse, honey. She really is."

"I hope Tollefson doesn't think so!" Janet said gravely. "If he did, he would stop at nothing. He's not a man who can stand losing, Tandy! He forced Dad off his range and then had him shot when he made trouble. He has a gunman who rides wherever he goes."

"I saw him." Meadows was serious. "Tom Passman's no bluffer. I know that. He doesn't remember me because I was just a kid when he last saw me, but I've seen him sling a gun, and he's fast."

"Are you having dinner with us? Dad will want

194

to see you even though it isn't like it used to be on the ranch."

He hesitated, searching her eyes. "I might come, Janet." His eyes wandered up the street toward where Passman was loitering. Are — are you married?"

"Married?" She was startled, but then her eyes crinkled with laughter. "Whatever gave you that idea?"

"Seems to be a fairly common practice" — he was grinning his relief — "when a girl gets to be your age. I figured I'd come back and see if you're still as dead set against a man who tramps around the country racing horses."

"Tandy," she said seriously, "you'll have to admit it wouldn't be much of a life for a girl, even though," she added reluctantly, "it might be exciting."

"It isn't so important where folks are," he commented, "as long as they are happy together."

"I've thought of that." She studied him. "Tandy, are you ever going to settle down? Haven't you enough of it yet?"

"Maybe. We'll see. I figured when I left I would never come back at all. Then I heard what happened to Jim Whitten and to your dad. Why, your father took me in when I was all shot up, and if you two hadn't cared for me, I would sure enough have passed in my checks. As for Whitten, he never made trouble for anybody. So I had to come back."

There was quick fear in her eyes now. "Don't

think about it, Tandy. Please don't. Nothing is worth what they could do to you. Tollefson's too strong, Tandy; nobody has a chance with him, and there's that awful Tom Passman."

"Sure. But why is he strong? Only because he has money, that's all. Suppose he lost it?"

"But how could he?"

"He could." Meadows squeezed her arm gently. "Believe me, honey, he could!"

Turning, he started down the street, aware that Tom Passman was watching him. He knew one reason for the man's curiosity. He was wondering if Meadows carried a gun, and if so, where it was. And if not, why not?

Snap was sitting on the wagon tongue when Tandy rode up to the camp in the creek bottom. Snap got to his feet and strolled out to meet Meadows, the shotgun in the crook of his arm. He was grinning expectantly. "You got a bet?" he asked softly.

Meadows nodded, smiling. "We sure have, Snap! And a lively hunch Tollefson would like nothing so much as to be safely out of it! We're going to have to be careful!" Meadows paused, then added:

"The man's no gambler. He's got a good horse, we know that. A mighty fast horse. We've got to hope ours is faster."

Snap nodded gravely. "You know I've seen that Lady Luck run, Mistuh Tandy. She's a mighty quick filly."

"Think she can beat Cholo Baby?"

Snap smiled. "Well, now. I reckon I'm some prejudiced about that! I never seen the horse I figured could beat our baby. But it will be a race, Mistuh Tandy! It sure will!"

The race was scheduled for the following Wednesday, three days away. By the time Meadows rode again to El Poleo, the town was buzzing with news of the bet. Tandy had done much to see the story got around, for the more who knew of it the less chance of Tollefson backing out. Yet the town was buzzing with more than that, for there was much speculation about Tandy Meadows, where he came from and where he got the money to make such a bet.

Nobody in town knew him but several had seen Janet Bates greet him like an old friend, and that in itself was puzzling. Art Tollefson was curious about that, and being the man he was, he went directly to the source, to Bates's small ranch forty miles north of El Poleo. Johnny Herndon, a Bates hand, was hazing a half-dozen cattle out of the brush, and his eyes narrowed when he saw Tollefson.

"You off your home range, Tollefson?" he said abruptly. "Or are you figurin' on pushin' us off this piece, too?"

Tollefson waved a hand. Yet his eyes had noted the grass and that some of it was subirrigated. It was an idea, at that. "Nothing like that," he replied shortly. "Just ridin' around a little. Saw a puncher down to El Poleo with some fine horses, a man named Meadows."

"Tandy Meadows?" Herndon had heard nothing of the bet, and he was instantly curious. "So he came back, did he? I sort of reckoned he would. Does he have some racin' stock with him?"

"Some, I reckon. Is he from around here?"

"Meadows? He's from nowhere. He rode in here one night over a year ago, shot to doll rags and barely hangin' to his horse. That was the first any of us ever saw of him. Gene Bates took him off his horse and they spent two months nursin' him back to health. Then he loafed around another month, sort of recuperatin'.

"Personally, I never figured he'd leave, for Janet sort of took to him, and the way they acted, it was mutual, but he finally pulled out."

"You said he'd been shot up? How did that happen? He doesn't even carry a gun now."

"No? Now, that's funny. They tell me he was some slick. I heard of him after he left here, but it was the story of some shootin' scrape down to Santa Fe before he drifted this way. Good two years ago. He never did say who shot him up, but some of us done some figurin' an' we reckoned it was the Alvarez gang. Story was they stole a bunch of horses off him, and that must be so. He got me to help him ride north and haze a bunch out of a canyon up there, and mighty fine stock.

"He'd evidently left them there when he was shot up, but he just had to close the gate as they were in a box canyon hideout with plenty of grass and water. They were somewhat wild but in fine shape."

"You mean the Alvarez gang had taken the horses there? Did you see any of them?"

Herndon shrugged, rolling a smoke. It was a bright, sunny morning and he had talked to nobody in three days. "Didn't figure I would. Meadows told me there wouldn't be any trouble, and he's the sort of man who would know.

"No, we saw hide nor hair of nobody. At the up end of that canyon there was an adobe, and Tandy advised me to stay away from it. But once I did get sort of close and there was somethin' white lyin' there that I'd swear was a skeleton."

"Has he got any money?"

"Who, Tandy?" Herndon chuckled. "I doubt it. He's a saddle tramp. Thinks of nothin' but what's the other side of the hill and racin' his horses. If he ever had more than a thousand dollars in his life it would surprise me."

Chapter 3
Trickery

Art Tollefson was a cautious man, and he had been very lacking in caution when he had allowed his pride to trap him into the bet with Meadows, but now he was doing a lot of serious thinking. The following morning he mounted up, and saying nothing to anyone, he rode north, avoiding the Bateses' range and heading for the area in which the box canyon had been.

From Herndon's comments it was not too hard to find, although had he not been expecting it, a man could have ridden by within a dozen yards and never guessed its existence. The bars were up, but he took them down and rode into a pleasant little canyon, grass covered and shady with probably two hundred acres of rich land in the bottom, and a good spring at the head of it.

Nearing the adobe he rode more cautiously, and when several yards away, he drew up. Obviously, no one had been this close to the cabin for a long time, and Herndon's surmise had been correct. It was a skeleton.

Buzzards had stripped the bones bare since, but the chaps and gun belts remained, their leather stiff as board from weathering. Not far from the bones lay a rusted six shooter.

Tollefson trailed his reins and walked up to the door. He stopped there, his mouth suddenly dry. Here three men had died, and they had died hard. The table was turned on its side and nearby lay another skeleton, face down on the dirt floor. Another slumped in the corner with a round hole over the eye, and the third was sprawled under some fallen slickers in a corner.

The scene was not hard to reconstruct. They had been surprised here by a man who had walked in through the doorway. The fourth man had evidently been drawn by the gunfire or had come up later. It was a very thoughtful man who turned his horse toward El Poleo somewhat later. If Tandy Meadows had walked away from that cabin alive, he was nobody with whom to play games. The sooner Passman knew, the better.

At four o'clock on the afternoon of the day before the race, Tandy Meadows watched Snap prepare an early supper. He was as good a hand with food as with horses, and he worked swiftly and surely, yet his eyes were restless and he was obviously on edge. "You reckon he'll make trouble, Boss?"

"I'd almost bet on it," Meadows replied, "but you can't tell. His pride might keep him from it. He figures Lady Luck will win, I know, but he's not a gambling man, and he'd like to be sure."

"You'd better watch that Passman," Snap advised. "He's a bad man."

Tandy nodded. He was the last man in the world to take Tom Passman lightly, for he had seen him throw a gun, and the man was deadly. Moreover, he was a tough man with a lot of pride in his skill, no braggart, and no four flusher. Only death itself would stop his guns.

Cholo Baby, a beautiful sorrel, lifted her head and whinnied softly as he approached. She was fifteen hands high, with wide-spaced and intelligent eyes. She stretched her velvety nose toward his hand and he touched her lightly. "How's it, girl? You ready to run for me tomorrow?"

Baby nudged him with her nose and Tandy grinned. "I doubt if you ever lived a day when you didn't feel like running, Cholo. And I hope there never is!"

He strolled back to the wagon, his eyes alert and searching the mountainside, the willows and the trail. He ate without talking, restless and disturbed despite himself. So far everything had been too quiet. Much too quiet.

He could neither rest nor relax. A hint of impending danger hung over the camp and he roved restlessly about. Snap seemed to feel it, too, and even the horses were alert as if they sensed something in the air. Of course, Tandy reflected, if anything happened to Cholo Baby, he could ride Khari, the half-Morgan, half-Arabian horse he usually rode. Not so fast as Cholo Baby over the quarter, but still a fast horse for one with so much staying power.

He still carried his rawhide riata. He was a California rider, and like them he valued the use of the riata, and was amazingly proficient with it. The California riders always used rawhide riatas of great length, and used them with such skill they were almost part of them. Suddenly, Tandy Meadows stopped. Hard upon the trail he heard the pounding hooves of a hard-ridden horse!

Snap was on his feet, leaning against the off wheel of the wagon, his shotgun resting over the corner of the wagon box to cover the trail. Tandy fell back near the wagon where his Winchester stood and waited, his lips tight, his eyes cool. Yet when the rider drew nearer he saw it was Janet Bates.

She drew up sharply and dropped to the ground. "Oh, Tandy!" Her face was pale. "What have you *done?* I just heard today you'd made a bet with Tollefson for his whole ranch! Tandy, you know you haven't that kind of money! If you lose, what will you do? One man did fail to pay off Tollefson once and he had been lashed to a tree and whipped by Tom Passman! He'd kill you, Tandy!"

Meadows smiled at her anxiety. "So you do worry about me? You do like me a little, then?"

"Be serious." Her eyes flashed. In the dusk she seemed even more lovely than ever. "You're in trouble, and you don't even know it. Lady Luck always wins, Tandy. He'll kill you!"

"He must have figured my bet was all right," Meadows replied. "Clevenger backed me."

"Oh, I know, Tandy! But you fooled him somehow. I just know you fooled him! If you don't win, what will you do?"

"I'll win," he replied simply. "I've got to win. I've got to win for you, Janet, and for your father and Jim Whitten. I came back here to force Tollefson out of the country, and I'll not rest until I do! Your dad was mighty kind to me when I was all shot up and dyin'. Without you two I'd not be here, so when I heard of what had happened, I figured this out. I'd heard of Lady Luck, and I knew Tollefson was a mighty big-headed and stubborn man, so I deliberately worked on his pride."

"That isn't all I heard," Janet persisted quickly. "Tollefson was up near our ranch twice. He talked to Johnny about you, asking all sorts of questions. He seemed very curious about how you'd been wounded that time, and the next day Johnny Herndon saw him riding north toward the box canyon where you left your horses that time."

Meadows scowled. What did that mean, anyway? The Alvarez gang had been notorious outlaws, and the killing of them would be considered a public service. Or would have at the time. Yet with such information a man of his influence might find some way to do him harm.

"Boss," Snap's voice was urgent, "somebody comin'."

Tandy Meadows turned and watched the horsemen. There were four in the group and one of them he recognized instantly as Tom Passman. When they drew nearer he saw that another was

Fulton, while the two riding with them were Sheriff George Lynn and his deputy Rube Hatley.

"Meadows," Lynn said, "we rode out here after you. You've got to come back to town and answer a few questions."

"Always glad to answer questions, Sheriff. Can't I answer them here?"

"No." Lynn's voice was testy. "You can answer them in my office. There's a place for such things and this isn't it!"

"All right, Sheriff," Meadows agreed. "But how about lettin' Hatley stay here to guard my horses?"

Lynn hesitated, disturbed by the request. It was reasonable enough, but when Art Tollefson had told him what to do, George Lynn had been reasonably certain what lay behind it. If he left Hatley he would be defeating the purpose of the trip. "Sorry," he replied abruptly, "I need Hatley with me!"

"Then of course you'll be responsible for my horses?" Meadows persisted. "I don't think they should be left alone."

"They'll be safe enough." Lynn was growing angry. "The responsibility is your own. Are you coming," he asked sharply, "or do we take you?"

"Why, I'm coming, Sheriff. I've never suggested anything to the contrary." He put his foot into the stirrup, then swung aboard Khari. "Snap," he said loudly, "if any varmints come around, don't take chances. Shoot to kill." Then he added, "You'll be perfectly safe because no-body would be fool enough to come near racin' stock on the night before a race. So don't forget, shoot to kill!"

"Sure thing, boss. I got me a shotgun loaded for bear!"

Nothing more was said as they rode back to town. Several times Tandy saw Passman watching him, but when they reached town only a few loafers noticed them ride down the street to the sheriff's office.

Inside, Lynn came to the point at once. "I've brought you in to ask you questions about a shootin' scrape, some time back."

"Why, sure!" Meadows dropped into a chair. "I didn't figure Tollefson rode all the way up to that canyon for nothing. He must be really worried if he's tryin' this hard to find a way out of his bet. But aren't you and Passman buckin' a stacked deck? Who will you work for if I win?"

"I work for the county!" Lynn said sharply. "That horse race has nothing to do with this inquiry!"

"Of course not! That's why Fulton and Passman were with you, Sheriff! Because the race has nothing to do with it! That's why you waited to bring me in until the night before the race! I hope somebody tries to bother those horses to-night! Snap's a whiz with a shotgun!"

He turned his head. "Passman came along hopin' I'd make some wrong play so he could plug me."

Passman's eyes were flat and gray. "You talk a lot," he said shortly, "but can you shoot?"

Lynn waved an irritated hand. "Who were those hombres you shot up north?"

"I shot?" Meadows looked mildly astonished. "Why, Sheriff, I didn't say I shot anybody. I did hear something about the Alvarez gang catching some lead over some horses they stole, but beyond that I'm afraid I don't remember much about it."

"You deny you shot them? You deny the fight?"

"I don't deny anything, and I don't admit anything." Tandy's voice was cool. "If you're planning to arrest me, by all means do it. Also, get me a lawyer down here, then either file charges against me or turn me loose. This whole proceeding, Sheriff, is highly irregular. All you have is Tollefson's word that he saw some skeletons somewhere. Or some dead men, or some bullet holes, or something. You know that I was wounded about the same time, but even if they were not horse thieves, you'd have a tough time proving any connection."

Lynn was uneasy. This was the truth and he knew it, but this was what Tollefson wanted, and what he wanted he got. Yet for almost three hours he persisted in asking questions, badgering Meadows with first one and then another, and trying to trap him. Yet he got nowhere. Finally, he got to his feet. "All right, you can go. If I want any more questions answered, I'll send for you."

207

Meadows got to his feet and let his eyes, suddenly grown cold, go over the four men. "All right, Sheriff, I'm always glad to answer questions, but get this: if anything has happened to my horses while I was in here, I'm coming back, and I'll be looking for each and every one of you.

"And that, Lynn," his eyes turned to the sheriff, "goes for you, sheriff or no sheriff! I'm a law-abiding man, and have always been, but if you've conspired with that fat-headed Tollefson to keep my horse out of that race, and through it harm comes to my horses, you'd better start packing a gun for me! Get that?"

George Lynn's face whitened and he involuntarily drew back. Worriedly, he glanced at Fulton and Passman for support. Fulton was pale as himself, and Passman leaned against the wall, nonchalantly rolling a cigarette. Rube Hatley stood near the door, his position unchanged. Meadows turned and walked past him, scarcely hearing the whispered, "Luck!" from Rube.

After he was gone, Lynn stared at Fulton. "Harry, what will we do?"

Rube Hatley chuckled. "Only one thing you can do, Sheriff. You can light a shuck out of the country or you can die. Either way, I don't care. I wanted no part of this yellow-bellied stunt, and if they were my horses I'd shoot you on sight."

"Passman?" Lynn was almost pleading. "You're the gunslinger."

Passman shrugged. "When I get my orders. Until then I don't make a move." He turned on

208

his heel and walked out into the night.

Lynn stared at Fulton. "Harry," he begged, "you know. What did they do?"

"Do?" Fulton's hand shook as he lighted his smoke. "Tollefson's too smart to pull anything too raw. He just had some of the boys take those horses out and run them over the desert for three hours, that's all! By daylight those horses will be so stiff and stove up they wouldn't be able to walk that quarter, let alone run it!"

"What about the black boy?"

Fulton shrugged. "That's another story. Who cares about him?"

"Meadows might."

"Yeah." Fulton was thoughtful. "He might at that. But you can be sure of one thing, after the runnin' his horses got this night, through cactus, brush, and rocks, they'll do no running tomorrow. I can promise you that! You leave the rest to Passman!"

"Did Tollefson actually *see* those skeletons?"

"He sure did." Fulton's voice was dry, emotionless. "And from what he said, if that was Tandy Meadows who walked into that shack after the Alvarez boys, he's got nerve enough to crawl down a hole after a nest full of rattlers, believe me!"

Chapter 4
Gilt-Edged Collateral

Morning dawned bright and still, and for the better part of two hours it remained bright and still, and then the boys from the ranches began to show up in El Poleo. Hard-riding youngsters, most of them, with here and there older men whose eyes were careful and wary with the sense of trouble.

Buckboards, a fringed surrey, a Conestoga wagon, and many horseback riders, all coming in for the races, and all curious about what would happen. Some had heard there had been trouble the night before, but what or when, they did not know.

Art Tollefson came in about noon. The covered wagon stood in the creek bottom disconsolate and alone. No horses were in sight, nor movement of any kind. His lips thinned with cruelty and his eyes were bright with triumph and satisfaction. Try to buck Art Tollefson, would they!

He was walking into the saloon when he saw a buckboard draw up between two buildings, and Gene Bates and Jim Whitten got down. His lips tightened and he walked on into the saloon.

The usual jovial laughter stilled as he entered.

210

With a wave of the hand he invited all and sundry to join him at the bar. Each year this was his custom at this time, but now there was no concerted rush for the bar.

This time, not a man moved.

Impatiently, he stared around the room but all eyes avoided his. Then Fulton stepped to the bar followed by several of his own Flying T riders. His face and neck crimson, Tollefson stared down at his drink, his jaw set hard.

Gene Bates and Jim Whitten walked into the saloon and to the bar. "Tollefson's buyin'," the bartender explained hurriedly.

"Not our drinks!" Bates's voice was flat. "I'll drink with no man who hires his killin' done and hires other men to ruin a man's horses so he loses a race!"

Tollefson whirled. The truth was hard to take, he found. "Who said that?" he demanded. "That's a lie!"

Bates faced him. The white-haired old man's blue eyes were fierce. "Better back up on that, Tollefson," he advised coldly. "Passman's not here to do your shootin' for you this time!"

Tollefson's fingers stiffened, and for an instant he seemed about to draw, but at Fulton's low-voiced warning, he turned back to the bar.

Sheriff George Lynn pushed through the doors and walked to the bar. He spoke under his breath to Tollefson. "They did it all right! They ran those horses half to death! I passed 'em out on the flat not thirty minutes ago, and a worse lookin' bunch you never did see! I couldn't get close, but it was close enough!"

"What will Meadows do now?" Fulton asked, low voiced.

Rube Hatley had come in. He overheard Fulton's remark and leaned both elbows on the bar. "Do?" Rube chuckled without humor. "If I were you hombres I'd do one of two things. I'd start ridin' or start shootin'!"

The course was the same straightaway course they had used for this race for several years. There were several two-twenty and three-thirty races to be run off before the quarter races began.

Tollefson watched nervously, his eyes roving the crowd. He saw neither Tandy Meadows nor Snap. Janet Bates rode in with Johnny Herndon, and they joined her father and Jim Whitten.

Fulton sat with Tollefson and Sheriff Lynn, and the last to arrive was Tom Passman. He dismounted but kept free of the crowd. Tollefson noted with relief that he was wearing two guns, something he rarely did. When he walked to the edge of the track, people moved away from him.

The quarter horse race was announced, and Tollefson touched his lips uneasily with his tongue as he watched Lady Luck walking into place in the line. Three other horses were entered in this race and they all showed up. All but one had been beaten by the Lady in previous races, and Tollefson began to breathe easier.

What a fool he had been to take such a chance! Well, it was over now, and he was safe. But where was Meadows?

Fulton grabbed his arm. *"Look!"* he gasped. "Look there!"

Another horse had moved into line, a sorrel, and beautifully made. The rider on the last horse was Snap, Meadows's Negro rider.

Tollefson's face flushed, then went white. He started forward, but stopped suddenly. Gene Bates was standing in front of him with a shotgun. "Let's let 'em run," Bates suggested. "You keep your place!"

Tollefson drew back, glancing around desperately. Sheriff Lynn had disappeared, but Rube Hatley loafed nearby. "Do something, man!" Tollefson insisted.

"For what?" Hatley grinned at him, his eyes hard. "Nobody's busted any law that I can see. That shotgun's in the hollow of his arm. Nobody says he can't carry it there."

Now the horses were moving together toward the far end of the course. As in a trance, Art Tollefson watched them go, watched most of all that sorrel with the squat black rider. Suddenly, he felt sick. If that horse won, he was through, *through!* It was unthinkable.

He turned sharply. "Tom!" he said. Passman looked around, his eyes level and gray. "When you see him! And there's a bonus in it for you!"

Passman nodded but made no other reply. Fulton felt a constriction in his chest. He had heard Tollefson order men beaten, cattle driven off, homes burned, but this was the first time he had actually heard him order a man killed. Yet nowhere was there any sign of Tandy Meadows.

Tollefson sat his horse where he could see the race, the full length of the course. His eyes went now to the far end where the horses were lining up now, and his heart began to pound. His fingers on the saddle horn were relaxed and powerless. Suddenly, the full impact of his bet came home to him, and he realized, almost for the first time, what losing would mean.

How had he ever been such a fool? Such an utter and complete fool? How had he been trapped into such a situation?

His thoughts were cut sharply off by the crack of a pistol, and his heart gave a tremendous leap as he saw the horses lunge into a dead run. Lady Luck had seemed almost to squat as the pistol cracked, and then bounded forward and was down the track running like a scared rabbit.

Tollefson, his breath coming hoarsely, stood in his stirrups, his agonized stare on the charging horses, and suddenly he realized he was shouting his triumph, for the Lady was well off and running beautifully. Then, even as he cheered, a sorrel shot from the group behind the Lady and swooped down upon her!

His pulse pounding, his eyes bulging with fear and horror, he saw that rusty streak of horse come up behind the Lady, saw its head draw abreast, then the nose was at the Lady's shoulder, and the Lady was running like something possessed, as if she knew what great change rode with her. Tollefson was shouting madly now, almost in a frenzy, for out there with those running horses was everything he owned, everything he had fought for, burned for, killed for. And now that sorrel with its crouching black rider was neck and neck with the Lady, and then with the finish line only a length away the sorrel seemed to give a great leap and shot over the finish line, winner by half a length!

Tollefson sagged back in his saddle, staring blindly down the hill. Tricked — tricked and beaten. Lady Luck was beaten. He was beaten. He was through, finished!

Then he remembered Tom Passman, and saw him standing down by the finish line, away from him. *Passman!* Tollefson's eyes suddenly sharpened. He could still win! Passman could kill them! He could kill Meadows, Whitten, Bates! Anyone who fought or resisted him! He would turn his riders loose on the town, he would —

Then a voice behind him turned him cold and still inside. "Well, you lost, Tollefson. You've got until sundown to get out of the country. You can load your personal belongings, no more. You can take a team and a buckboard. Get moving!"

Passman seemed to have heard. He turned slowly, and he was looking at them now from forty yards away. In a daze, Tollefson saw Tandy Meadows step out toward the gunman, holding in his hands nothing but the rawhide riata.

Tom Passman crouched a little, his eyes riveted on Meadows, his mind doing a quick study. If he drew and killed an unarmed man, there was a chance not even Tollefson could save him. Yet was Meadows unarmed? At what point might he not suddenly flash a gun from his shirtfront or waistband?

Meadows took another step, switching the rope in his hands with seeming carelessness. Again Passman's eyes searched Meadows's clothing for a suspicious bulge, and saw none. Surely, the man would not come down here without a weapon? It was beyond belief. "What's the matter, Tom?" Meadows taunted. "Yellow?"

As he spoke, his hands flipped, and as Passman's hands swept down for his guns he saw something leap at him like a streak of light. He threw up a hand, tried to spring aside, but that rawhide riata loop snapped over his shoulders and whipped taut even as his hands started to lift the guns, and he was jerked off balance.

He staggered, trying desperately to draw a gun, but his arms were pinned to his sides. Meadows took two running steps toward him, throwing another loop of the rope over his shoulders that fell to his ankles. He jerked hard and the gunman fell, hitting hard in the dust. He struggled to get up, and Tandy jerked him from his feet again. Tandy stood off, smiling grimly.

Then, stepping in quickly, he jerked the guns from Passman's holsters and tossed them aside. Springing back, he let Passman fight his way free of the noose. As the loop dropped from the gunman, he wheeled on Meadows, and Tandy struck him across the mouth with the back of his hand.

It was deliberate, infuriating. Passman went blind with rage and rushed. A left smeared his lips and a roundhouse right caught him on the ear. He staggered sideways, his ears ringing. Meadows walked into him then and slugged two wicked underhand punches into the gunman's body. Passman sagged and went down, landing on his knees.

Tandy jerked him erect, struck him again in the stomach, and ignoring the futile punches the man threw, stepped back and smashed him full in the mouth with a right. Passman went down again.

Bloody and battered, he lay gasping on the ground. Meadows stood over him. "Tom," he said coldly, "I could have killed you. You never saw the day you were as fast as I am. But I don't want to kill men, Tom. Not even you. Now get out of the country! If you ever come north of the river again, I'll hunt you down and kill you! Start *moving!*"

Tandy stepped back, coiling his rope. He glanced around. Tollefson was gone, and so was Fulton.

Rube Hatley gestured toward Passman. "He means it, Tom," he said, "and so do I. I'd have run you out of here months ago if it hadn't been for Tollefson and Lynn. Take his advice and don't come back, because I may not be any faster than you, Tom, but if you ever ride this way again, you've got me to kill, and I sort of think we'd go together!"

Hatley glanced at Tandy. "You had me fooled. What happened to your horses?"

"Janet and Snap figured something would happen, so they drove them back into the hills a mile or so, and then they moved in a bunch of half broke Flying T broomtails down on that meadow. In the dark they never guessed they were drivin' some of their own remuda!"

Janet came up to Tandy, smiling gravely, her eyes lighted with something half affection and half humor. "I was glad to help. I thought if you won this race you might settle down."

Meadows shrugged, grinning. "I don't see any way out of it with a ranch to manage and a wife to support."

Janet stared suspiciously from Meadows to Clevenger. "Now tell me," she insisted. "What would you have done if Cholo Baby had lost? How could you have paid up?"

The banker looked sheepish. "Well, ma'am, I reckon I'd have had to pay off. That was my money backing him."

"*Yours?*" she was incredulous. "Without collateral?"

"No, ma'am!" Clevenger shook his head decisively. "He had collateral! In the banking business a man's got to know what's good security and what isn't! What he showed me was plumb good enough for any old horseman like myself. It was Cholo Baby's pedigree!

"Why, ma'am, that Cholo Baby was sired by

218

old Dan Tucker, one of the finest quarter horse stallions of them all! He was a half brother to Peter McCue, who ran the quarter in twenty-one seconds!

"Like I say, ma'am, a banker has to know what's good collateral and what ain't! Why, a man what knows horses could no more fail to back that strain than he could bet against his own mother!

"And look," he said grinning shrewdly. "Was it good collateral, or wasn't it? Who *won?*"

LONG RIDE HOME

Before him rolled the red and salmon unknown, the vast, heat-waved unreality of the raw desert, broken only by the jagged crests of the broken bones of upthrust ledges. He saw the weird cacti and the tiny puffs of dust from the hooves of his grulla, but Tensleep Mooney saw no more.

Three days behind him was the Mexican border, what lay ahead he had no idea. Three days behind him lay the Rangers of Texas and Arizona, and a row of graves, some new buried, of men he had killed. But Tensleep Mooney of the fast gun and the cold eye was southbound for peace, away from the fighting, the bitterness, the struggle. He was fleeing not the law alone, but the guns of his enemies and the replies his own must make if he stayed back there.

Here not even the Apache rode. Here no peon came, and rarely even the Indians. This was a wild and lonely land, born of fire and tempered with endless sunlight, drifting dust-devils and the bald and brassy sky. Sweat streaked his dust-caked shirt, and there were spots flushed red beneath his squinted eyes, and pinkish desert dust in the dark stubble of his unshaven jaws.

Grimly, he pointed south, riding toward something he knew not what. In his pocket, ten silver pesos; in his canteen, a pint of brackish water remaining; in the pack on the stolen burro, a little sowbelly, some beans, rice, and enough ammunition to fight.

Behind him the Carrizal Mountains, behind him the green valleys of the Magdalena, and back along the line, a black horse dead of a rifle bullet, his own horse lying within a half minute's buzzard flight of the owner of the horse he now rode, a bandit who had been too optimistic for his health. And behind him at Los Chinos, a puzzled peon who had sold a mule and beans to a hard-faced Yanqui headed south.

Mooney had no destination before him. He was riding out of time, riding out of his world into any other world. What lay behind him was death wherever he rode, a land where the law sought him, and the feuding family of his enemies wanted vengeance for their horse-thieving relatives he had killed.

The law, it seemed, would overlook the killing of a horse thief. It would even overlook the killing of a pair of his relatives if they came hunting you, but when it came to the point of either eliminating the males of a big family or being eliminated oneself, they were less happy. Tensleep Mooney had planted seven of them and had been five months ducking bullets before the Rangers closed in; and now, with discretion, Mooney took his valor south of the border.

Two days had passed in which he saw but one lonely rancho; a day since he came across any living thing except buzzards and lizards and an occasional rattler. He swung eastward, toward the higher mountains, hunting a creek or a water hole where he could camp for the night, and with luck, for a couple of days rest. His stock was gaunt and he was lean in the ribs and hollow cheeked.

The country grew rougher, the cacti thicker, the jagged ridges sloped up toward the heights of the mountains. And then the brush was scattered but head high, and then he saw a patch of greener brush ahead and went riding toward it, sensing water in the quickened pace of his grulla.

Something darted through the brush, and he shucked his gun with an instinctive draw that would have done credit to Wes Hardin — but he pushed on. He wanted water and he was going to have it if he had to fight for it.

The something was an Indian girl, ragged, thin and wide-eyed. She crouched above a man who lay on the sand, a chunk of rock in her hand, waiting at bay with teeth bared like some wild thing.

Mooney drew his horse to a stop and holstered his gun. She was thin, emaciated. Her cheekbones were startling against the empty cheeks and sunken eyes. She was barefoot, and the rags she wore covered a body that no man would have looked at twice. On the sand at her feet lay an old Indian, breathing hoarsely. One leg was wrapped in gruesomely dirty rags, and showed blood.

"What's the matter, kid?" he said in hoarse English. "I won't hurt you."

225

She did not relent, waiting, hopeless in her courage, ready to go down fighting. It was a feeling that touched a responsive chord in Tensleep, of the Wyoming Mooneys. He grinned and swung to the ground, holding a hand up, palm outward. "Amigo," he said, hesitantly. His stay in Texas had not been long and he knew little Spanish and had no confidence in that. "Me amigo," he said, and he walked up to the fallen man.

The man's face was gray with pain, but he was conscious. He was Indian, too. Tarahumara, Mooney believed, having heard of them. He dropped beside the old man and gently began to remove the bandage. The girl stared at him, then began to gasp words in some heathen, unbelievable language.

Mooney winced when he saw the wound. A bullet through the thigh. And it looked as ugly as any wound he had seen in a long time. Turning to the trees, Mooney began to gather dry sticks. When he started to put them together for a fire the girl sprang at him wildly and began to babble shrill protest, pointing off to the west as she did so. "Somebody huntin' you, is there?" Tensleep considered that, looked at the man, the girl, and considered himself, then he chuckled. "Don't let it bother you, kid," he said. "If we don't fix this old man up fast, he'll die. Maybe it's too late now. An'," here he chuckled again, "if they killed all of us, they wouldn't accomplish much."

The fire was made of dry wood and there was

little smoke. He put water on to get hot. Then when the water was boiling he went to a creosote bush and got leaves from it and threw them into the water. The girl squatted on her heels and watched him tensely. When he had allowed the leaves to boil for a while, he bathed the wound in the concoction. He knew that some Indians used it for an antiseptic for burns and wounds. The girl watched him, then darted into the brush and after several minutes came back with some leaves which she dampened and then began to crush into a paste. The old man lay very still, his face more calm, his eyes on Mooney's face.

Tensleep looked at the wide face, the large soft eyes that could no doubt be hard on occasion, and the firm mouth. This was a man — he had heard many stories of the endurance of these Tarahumara Indians. They would travel for fabulous miles without food, they possessed an unbelievable resistance to pain in any form. When the wound was thoroughly bathed, the girl moved forward with the paste and signified that it should be bound on the wound. He nodded, and with a tinge of regret he ripped up his last white shirt — the only one he had owned in three years — and bound the wound carefully. He was just finishing it when the girl caught his arm. Her eyes were wide with alarm, but he saw nothing. And then, as he listened, he heard horses drawing nearer and he got to his feet and slid his Winchester from its scabbard. His horse had stopped among the uptilted rocks that surrounded the water hole.

There were three of them, a well-dressed man with a thin, cruel face and two hard-faced vaqueros. "Ah!" The leader drew up. He looked down at the old Indian and said, *"Perro!"* Then his hand dropped to his gun and Tensleep Mooney drew.

The Mexican stopped, his hand on his own gun, looking with amazement into the black and steady muzzle of Tensleep's Colt. A hard man himself he had seen many men draw a pistol, but never a draw like this. His eyes studied the man behind the gun and he did not like what he saw. Tensleep Mooney was honed down and hard, a man with wide shoulders, a once broken nose, and eyes like bits of gray slate.

"You do not understand," the Mexican said coolly. "This man is an Indio. He is nothing. He is a dog. He is a thief."

"Where I come from," Mooney replied, "we don't shoot helpless men. An' we don't run Injuns to rags when they're afoot an' helpless. We," his mouth twisted wryly, "been hard on our own Injuns, but mostly they had a fightin' chance. I think this hombre deserves as much."

"You are far from other gringos," the Mexican suggested, "and I am Don Pedro," he waved a hand, "of the biggest hacienda in one hundred miles. The police, the soldiers, all of them come when I speak. You stop me now and there will not be room enough in this country for you to hide, and then we shall see how brave you are."

"That's as may be," Mooney shrugged, his eyes hard and casual. "You can see how big my feet are right now if you three want to have at it. I'll holster my gun, an' then you can try, all three of you. Of course," Mooney smiled a pleasant, Irish smile, "you get my first shot, right through the belly."

Don Pedro was no fool. It was obvious to him that even if they did kill the gringo that it would do nothing for Don Pedro, for the scion of an ancient house would be cold clay upon the Sonora desert. It was a most uncomfortable thought, for Don Pedro had a most high opinion of the necessity for Don Pedro's continued existence.

"You are a fool," he said coldly. He spoke to his men and swung his horse.

"An' you are not," Mooney said, "if you keep ridin'."

Then they were gone and he turned to look at the Indians. They stared at him as if he were a god, but he merely grinned and shrugged. Then his face darkened and he kicked the fire apart. "We got to move," he said, waving a hand at the desert, "away."

He shifted the pack on the burro and loaded the old man on the burro's back. "This may kill you, Old One," he said, "but unless I miss my guess, that hombre will be back with friends."

The girl understood at once, but refused to mount with him, striking off at once into the brush. "I hope you know where you're goin'," he said, and followed on, trusting to her to take them to a place of safety.

She headed south until suddenly they struck a long shelf of bare rock, then she looked up at him quickly, and gestured at the rock, then turned east into the deeper canyons. Darkness fell suddenly but the girl kept on weaving her way into a trackless country — and she herself seemed tireless.

His canteen was full, and when the girl stopped it was at a good place for hiding, but the *tinaja* was dry. He made coffee and the old man managed to drink some, then drank more, greedily.

He took out some of the meat and by signs indicated to the girl what he wanted. She was gone into the brush only a few minutes and then returned with green and yellow inflated stems. "Squaw cabbage!" he said. "I'll be durned! I never knowed that was good to eat!" He gestured to indicate adding it to the stew and she nodded vigorously. He peeled his one lone potato and added it to the stew.

All three ate, then rolled up and slept. The girl sleeping close to her father, but refusing to accept one of his blankets.

They started early, heading farther east. "Water?" he questioned.

She pointed ahead, and they kept moving. All day long they moved. His lips cracked, and the face of the old man was flushed. The girl still walked, plodding on ahead, although she looked in bad shape. It was late afternoon when she gestured excitedly and ran on ahead. When he caught up with her, she was staring at a water hole. It was brim full of water, but in the water floated a dead coyote.

"How far?" he asked, gesturing.

She shook her head, and gestured toward the sky. She meant either the next afternoon or the one following. In either case, there was no help for it. They could never last it out.

"Well, here goes," he said, and swinging down he stripped the saddle from the horse. Then while the girl made her father comfortable, he took the dead coyote from the water hole, and proceeded to build a fire, adding lots of dry wood. When he had a good pile of charcoal, he dipped up some of the water in a can, covered the surface to a depth of almost three inches with charcoal, and then put it on the fire. When it had boiled for a half hour, he skimmed impurities and the charcoal, and the water below looked pure and sweet. He dipped out enough to make coffee, then added charcoal to the remainder. When they rolled out in the morning the water looked pure and good. He poured it off into his canteen and they started on.

Now the girl at last consented to climb up behind him, and they rode on into the heat of a long day. Later, he swung down and walked, and toward night the girl slipped to the ground. And then suddenly the vegetation grew thicker and greener. The country was impossibly wild and lonely. They had seen nothing, for even the buzzards seemed to have given up.

Then the girl ran on ahead and paused. Tensleep walked on, then stopped dead still, staring in shocked amazement.

Before him, blue with the haze of late evening, lay a vast gorge, miles wide, and apparently, also miles deep! It stretched off to the southwest in a winding splendor, a gorge as deep as the Canyon of the Colorado, and fully as magnificent.

The girl led him to a steep path and unhesitatingly she walked down it. He followed. Darkness came and still she led on, and then suddenly he saw the winking eye of a fire! They walked on, and the girl suddenly called out, and after a minute there was an answering hail. And then they stopped on a ledge shaded by towering trees. Off to the left was the vast gorge; somewhere in its depths a river roared and thundered. Indians came out of the shadows, the firelight on their faces. Behind them was the black mouth of a cave, and something that looked like a wall with windows.

The old man was helped down from the burro and made comfortable. An old woman brought him a gourd dish full of stew and he ate hungrily. The Tarahumaras gathered around, unspeaking but watching. They seemed to be waiting for something, and then it came.

A man in a sombrero pushed his way through the Indians and stopped on the edge of the fire. Obviously an Indian also, he was dressed like a peon. "I speak," he said. "This man an' the girl say much thank you. You are good hombre."

"Thanks," Mooney said, "I was glad to do it. How do I get out of here?"

"No go." The man shook his head. "This man, Don Pedro, he will seek you. Here you must wait . . . here." He smiled. "He will not come. Here nobody will come."

Tensleep squatted beside the fire. That was all right, for awhile, but he had no desire to remain in this canyon for long. He could guess that the gorge would be highly unsafe for anyone who tried to enter without permission of the Tarahumaras. But to get out?

"How about downstream?" He pointed to the southwest. "Is there a way?"

"Si, but it is long an' ver' difficult. But you wait. Later will be time enough."

They brought him meat and beans, and he ate his fill for the first time in days. Squatting beside the fire he watched the Indians come and go, their dark, friendly eyes on his face, half-respectful, half-curious. The girl was telling them excitedly of all that happened, and from her excited gestures he could gather that the story of his facing down Don Pedro and his vaqueros was losing nothing in the telling.

For two days Mooney loitered in the gorge. Here and there along the walls were ledges where crops had been planted. Otherwise the Indios hunted, fished in the river, and went into the desert to find plants. Deeper in the canyon the growth was tropical. There were strange birds, jaguars, and tropical fruit. Once he descended with them, clear to the water's edge. It was a red and muddy stream, thinning down now as the rainy season ended, yet from marks on the walls he could see evidence that roaring torrents had raged through here, and he could understand why the Indios suggested waiting.

"Indio," he said suddenly on the third day, "I must go now. Ain't no use my stayin' here longer. I got to ride on."

The Indian squatted on his heels and nodded. "Where you go now?"

"South." He shrugged. "It ain't healthy for me back to the north."

"I see." Indio scratched under his arm. "You are bueno hombre, señor." From his shirt pocket he took a piece of paper on which an address had been crudely lettered. "Thees rancho," he said, "you go to there. Thees woman, she is Indio, like me. She ver' . . . ver' . . . how you say? Rico?"

"Yeah, I get you." Mooney shrugged. "All I want is a chance to lay around out of sight an' work a little for my grub. Enough to keep me goin' until I go back north." He rubbed his jaw. "Later, if I can get some cash I might go to Vera Cruz and take a boat for New Orleans, then back to Wyomin'. Yeah, that would be best."

Indio questioned him, and he explained, drawing a map in the dirt. The Indian nodded, grasping the idea quickly. He seemed one of the few who had been outside of the canyon for any length of time. He had, he said, worked for this woman to whom Mooney was to go. She was no longer young, but she was very wise, and her husband dead. Most of those who worked for her were Tarahumaras.

They left at daybreak, and the girl came to the door of the house-cave to motion to him. When he entered, the old Indian lay on the floor on a heap of skins and blankets. He smiled and held up a hand whose grip was surprisingly strong, and he spoke rapidly, then said something to the girl. When she came up to Mooney she held in her hands a skin-wrapped object that was unusually heavy. It was, Mooney gathered, a present. Awkwardly, he thanked them, then came out and mounted.

Once more his pack was rounded and full. Plenty of beans, some jerky, and some other things the Indians brought for him. All gathered together on the ledge to wave good-bye. Indio led him down a steep path, then into a branch canyon, and finally they started up.

It was daylight again before they reached the rancho for which they had started, and they had travelled nearly all day and night. Lost in the chaparral, Tensleep was astonished to suddenly emerge into green fields of cotton, beyond them were other fields, and some extensive orchards. And then to the wall-enclosed rancho itself.

The old woman had evidently been apprised of his coming, for she stood on the edge of the patio to receive him. She was short, like the other women of her people, but there was something regal in her bearing that impressed Mooney.

"How do you do?" she said, then smiled at his surprise. "Yes, I speak the English, although not well." Later, when he was bathed and shaved, he walked into the wide old room where she sat and she told him that when fourteen, she had been adopted by the Spanish woman who had lived here before her. She had been educated at home, then at school, and finally had married a young Mexican. He died when he was fifty, but she had stayed on at the ranch, godmother to her tribe.

Uneasily, Mooney glanced through the wide door at the long table that had been set in an adjoining room. "I ain't much on society, ma'am," he said. "I reckon I've lived in cow camps too long, among men-folks."

"It's nothing," she said. "There will come someone tonight whom I wish you to meet. Soon he goes north, over the old Smuggler's Crossing into the Chisos Mountains beyond the Rio Grande, and then to San Antonio. You can go with him, and so to your own country."

Suddenly, she started to talk to him of cattle and of Wyoming and Montana. Startled, he answered her questions and described the country. She must have been sixty at least, although Tarahumara women, he had noticed, rarely looked anywhere near their true ages, preserving their youth until very old. She seemed sharp and well

236

informed, and he gathered that she owned a ranch in Texas, and was thinking of sending a herd over the trail to Wyoming.

Suddenly, she turned on him. "Señor, you are a kind man. You are also a courageous one. You seem to know much of cattle and of your homeland. We of the Tarahumara do not forget quickly, but that does not matter now. You will take my herd north. You will settle it on land in Wyoming, buying what you need, you will be foreman of my ranch there."

Mooney was stunned. He started to protest, then relaxed. Why should he protest? He was a cattleman, she was a shrewd and intelligent woman. Behind her questioning there had been a lot of good sense, and certainly, it was a windfall for him. At twenty-seven he had nothing but his saddle, a horse and a burro — and experience.

"I am not a fool, señor," she said abruptly. "You know cattle, you know men. You have courage and consideration. Also, you know your own country best. There is much riches in cattle, but the grass of the northland fattens them best. This is good for you, I know that. It is also good for me. Who else do I know who knows your land of grass and snow?"

When he gathered his things together, she saw the skin-wrapped package. Taking it in her graceful brown fingers she cut the threads and lifted from the skin an image, not quite six inches high, of solid gold.

Mooney stared at it. Now where did those

Indians get anything like that?

"From the Caves," she told him when he spoke his thought. "For years we find them. Sometimes one here, sometimes one there. Perhaps at one time they were all together, somewhere. It is Aztec, I think, or Toltec. One does not know. It is ver' rich, this thing."

When dinner was over he stood on the edge of the patio with Juan Cabrizo. He was a slim, wiry young man with a hard, handsome face. "She is shrewd, the Old One," he said. "She makes money! She makes it like that!" He snapped his fingers. "I work for her as my father worked for old Aguila, who adopted her. She was ver' beautiful as a young girl." His eyes slanted toward Mooney. "This Don Pedro? You must be careful, si? Ver' careful. He is a proud and angry man. I think he knows where you are."

At daybreak they rode northeast, and Cabrizo led the way, winding through canyons, coming suddenly upon saddles, crossing ranges into long empty valleys. For two days they rode, and on the second night as they sat by a carefully shielded fire, Mooney nodded at it, "Is that necessary? You think this Don Pedro might come this far?"

Cabrizo shrugged. "I think only the Rio Grande will stop him. He is a man who knows how to hate, amigo, and you have faced him down before his vaqueros. For this he must have your heart."

There were miles of sun and riding, miles when

the sweat soaked his shirt and the dust caked his face and rimmed his eyes. And then there was a cantina at Santa Teresa.

Juan lifted a glass to him at the bar of the cantina. "Soon, señor, tomorrow perhaps, you will cross into your own country! To a happy homecoming!"

Tensleep Mooney looked at his glass, then tossed it off. It was taking a chance, going back into Texas, but still, he had crossed the border from Arizona, and they no doubt would not guess he was anywhere around. Moreover, he had crossed as an outlaw, now he returned as a master of three thousand head of cattle.

"*Señor!*" Cabrizo hissed. "Have a care! It is *he!*"

Tensleep Mooney turned slowly. Don Pedro had come in the door and with him were four men.

Mooney put down his glass and stepped swiftly around the table. Don Pedro turned to face him, squinting his eyes in the bright light. And then the barrel of Mooney's gun touched his belt and he froze, instantly aware. "You're a long ways from home, Don Pedro," he said. "You chasin' another Indian?"

"No, señor," Don Pedro's eyes flashed. "I chase you! And now I have caught you."

"Or I've caught you. Which does it look like?"

"I have fifty men!"

"An' if they make one move, you also have, like I warned you before, a bellyful of lead."

Don Pedro stood still, raging at his helplessness. His men stood around, not daring to move. "Perhaps you are right," he admitted coldly. "Because I am not so skillful with the gun as you."

"You have another weapon?"

"I?" Don Pedro laughed. "I like the knife, señor. I wish I could have you here with the knife, alone!"

Tensleep chuckled suddenly, the old lust for battle rising in his throat like a strong wine, stirring in his veins. "Why, sure! Tell your men we will fight here, with the knife. If I win, I am to go free."

Don Pedro stared at him, incredulous. "You would dare, señor?"

"Will they obey you? Is your word good?"

"My word?" Don Pedro's nostrils flared. "Will they obey me?" He wheeled on them, and in a torrent of Spanish told them what they would do.

Cabrizo said, "He tells them, amigo. He tells them true, but this you must not. It is a way you would die."

Coolly, Mooney shucked his gun belts and placed them on the bar beside Cabrizo. Then from a scabbard inside his belt he drew his bowie knife. "The gent that first used this knife," he said, "killed eight men with it without gettin' out of bed where he was sick. I reckon I can slit the gullet of one man!"

Don Pedro was tall, he was lean and wiry as a whip, and he moved across the floor like a dancer. Mooney grinned and his slate-gray eyes danced with a hard light.

Pedro stepped in quickly, light glancing off his knife blade, stepped in, then thrust! And Mooney caught the blade with his own bowie and turned it aside. Pedro tried again, and Mooney again caught the blade and they stood chest to chest, their knives crossed at the guard. Mooney laughed suddenly and exerting all the power in his big, work-hardened shoulders, thrust the Mexican away from him. Pedro staggered back, then fell to a sitting position.

Furious, he leaped to his feet and lunged, blind with rage. Mooney side-stepped, slipped, and hit the floor on his shoulder. Pedro sprang at him but Mooney came up on one hand and stabbed up. He felt the knife strike, felt it slide open in the stomach of Don Pedro, and then for one long minute their eyes held. Not a foot apart, Don Pedro's whole weight on the haft of Mooney's knife. "Bueno!" Don Pedro said hoarsely. "As God wills!" Slowly, horribly, he turned his eyes toward his men. "Go home!" he said in Spanish. "Go home to my brother. It was my word!"

Carefully, Tensleep Mooney lowered the body to the floor and withdrew the knife. Already the man was dead. "What kind of cussedness is it," he said, "that gets into a man? He had nerve enough." But remembering the Indian, he could find no honest regret for Pedro, only that this had happened.

"Come, amigo," Cabrizo said softly, "it is better we go. It is a long ride to Wyoming, no?"

"A long ride," Tensleep Mooney agreed, "an' I'll be glad to get home."

ABOUT LOUIS L'AMOUR

"I think of myself in the oral tradition — as a troubadour, a village taleteller, the man in the shadows of the campfire. That's the way I'd like to be remembered — as a storyteller. A good storyteller."

It is doubtful that any author could be as at home in the world recreated in his novels as Louis Dearborn L'Amour. Not only could he physically fill the boots of the rugged characters he wrote about, but he literally "walked the land my characters walk." His personal experiences as well as his lifelong devotion to historical research combined to give Mr. L'Amour the unique knowledge and understanding of people, events, and the challenge of the American frontier that became the hallmarks of his popularity.

Of French-Irish descent, Mr. L'Amour could trace his own family in North America back to the early 1600s and follow their steady progression westward, "always on the frontier." As a boy growing up in Jamestown, North Dakota, he absorbed all he could about his family's frontier heritage, including the story of his great-grandfather who was scalped by Sioux warriors.

Spurred by an eager curiosity and desire to broaden his horizons, Mr. L'Amour left home at the age of fifteen and enjoyed a wide variety of jobs including seaman, lumberjack, elephant handler, skinner of dead cattle, assessment miner, and an officer in the tank destroyers during World War II. During his "yondering" days he also circled the world on a freighter, sailed a dhow on the Red Sea, was shipwrecked in the West Indies and stranded in the Mojave Desert. He won fifty-one of fifty-nine fights as a professional boxer and worked as a journalist and lecturer. He was a voracious reader and collector of rare books. His personal library contained 17,000 volumes.

Mr. L'Amour "wanted to write almost from the time I could talk." After developing a widespread following for his many frontier and adventure stories written for fiction magazines, Mr. L'Amour published his first full-length novel, *Hondo*, in the United States in 1953. Every one of his more than 100 books is in print; there are nearly 230 million copies of his books in print worldwide, making him one of the bestselling authors in modern literary history. His books have been translated into twenty languages, and more than forty-five of his novels and stories have been made into feature films and television movies.

His hardcover bestsellers include *The Lonesome Gods*, *The* Walking Drum (his twelfth-century historical novel), *Jubal Sackett*, *Last of the Breed*, and *The Haunted Mesa*. His memoir, *Education of a Wandering Man*, was a leading bestseller in 1989.

The recipient of many great honors and

awards, in 1983 Mr. L'Amour became the first novelist ever to be awarded the Congressional Gold Medal by the United States Congress in honor of his life's work. In 1984 he was also awarded the Medal of Freedom by President Reagan.

Louis L'Amour died on June 10, 1988. His wife, Kathy, and their two children, Beau and Angelique, carry the L'Amour tradition forward with new books written by the author during his lifetime.

The employees of G.K. Hall hope you have enjoyed this Large Print book. All our Large Print titles are designed for easy reading, and all our books are made to last. Other G.K. Hall books are available at your library, through selected bookstores, or directly from us.

For information about titles, please call:

(800) 257-5157

To share your comments, please write:

Publisher
G.K. Hall & Co.
P.O. Box 159
Thorndike, ME 04986